David Howarth, Henry Weston Taylor

The Valley of Gold

A Tale of the Saskatchewan

David Howarth, Henry Weston Taylor

The Valley of Gold
A Tale of the Saskatchewan

ISBN/EAN: 9783337364175

Printed in Europe, USA, Canada, Australia, Japan

Cover: Foto ©Andreas Hilbeck / pixelio.de

More available books at **www.hansebooks.com**

*"Bridges are all burned. To-morrow I
begin teaching—where do you think?"*

The Valley of Gold
A Tale of the Saskatchewan

BY DAVID HOWARTH

FRONTISPIECE BY
H. WESTON TAYLOR

A. L. BURT COMPANY
Publishers New York
Published by arrangement with Fleming H. Revell Company
Printed in U. S. A.

TO MY MOTHER

Contents

I

HEAVY ODDS

The east wind blew furiously, beating gray sheets down the streaming panes. Along the village street flowed a turbid torrent, the squalid wash of an "old-timer-three-days'-blow" from the Great Lakes. Threshing was hung up. Every wheel was stopped for a thousand miles across the prairies.

Sparrow's pool-room was a cavern of smoke. Through the blue-ringed mists of tobacco moved the unkempt silhouettes of boisterous threshermen. Suddenly over the hubbub rose a jeering cry.

Ned Pullar leaned down and knocked the ashes out of his briar. His immobile face gave no sign that the cry was an insulting challenge. Opening his knife he slowly scooped out the bowl of his pipe. Tapping the inverted briar on the palm of his hand, he proceeded leisurely to fill in the tobacco. This act duly completed, he turned about and looked McClure in the face. In his eyes was a faint twinkle, but he elected to hold his tongue. His deliberate silence provoked his tormentor. Hitherto McClure had addressed him in a low tone. Now his great voice rose above the chatter of the players and the noise of the crashing balls.

"Come, Pullar!" he sneered. "You're yellow. How about odds?"

Play ceased and all eyes turned on the two men.

"Pull easy, Rob!" adjured some partisan of McClure's. "He's soft in the mouth."

The crowd raised applauding guffaws.

"Naw, it's the blind staggers, pards," cried a smooth voice. "Watch his blinkers."

The immoderate laugh of the crowd had a curiously menacing note.

Pullar's blinkers were not blinking, however. He held

McClure's eyes with a level glance.

Thrusting hands to hips akimbo McClure cried insolently:

"S-s-stumped! You quitter!"

Pullar was still silent. His clear eye was taking in the situation. McClure was plainly bent on baiting him and his purpose was beginning to dawn on the Valley boss. A quick survey of the room discovered to him the presence of nine of McClure's men. He could see them moving about into position to cut off all egress from the one door. Not a man of his own gang was in sight and the two or three outsiders were not promising allies. The stench of liquor and the savage flashing of wild eyes warned him of their fell intention. In the swift process of his thought he realized that they were about to pull him down and "jump" him with the unspeakable savagery of drunken fools. He was trapped. With every sense alert he went ahead imperturbably preparing to light up.

Drawing a wad of bills from his pocket McClure thrust them under Pullar's nose.

"Five hundred bucks!" he challenged. "Five hundred little bucks to lay against you two to one that we can lick the Valley Outfit in a thirty day run any old time you want to take it on. No time like the present, Pullar!"

Ned Pullar stood straight and immense, a muscular figure in overalls and smock. His fresh, youthful face looked almost innocently from under the peak of his cap. His eyes were serious for an instant, then released an amused smile.

"Rob McClure!" he said quietly. "You are developing an interesting humour. Three times to-day you have flaunted this trifling wager in my face. It means nothing to me—nothing more than do you yourself, Robbie, mon, or your engaging gang."

The mocking tone provoked a swift change in McClure. His eyes narrowed to slits that gleamed evilly. The rush of passion rendered him impotently mute. Backing their boss with yells of rage the gang moved menacingly toward the speaker. Suddenly above the foul oaths rang out a voice. It was one of the outsiders who had slipped unnoticed to the door. With his hand on the knob he called out:

"Hold 'em, Ned. I'll fetch the Valley Outfit mighty quick."

There was a rush toward him, but he dashed out of the door and away.

Then followed an instant move toward the solitary and defiant figure of the Valley boss.

"Halt! You drunken dogs!" cried Pullar in a voice that effected his purpose.

Pausing, the crowd eyed their quarry cautiously, warned by the terrible flame leaping from the eyes where but a moment before glimmered a whimsical smile. Holding his pipe to his lips with a match ready to light, he addressed them quietly.

"I was getting ready," said he, "to hit the trail for The Craggs when McClure worked himself up over this bet. I'm not interested in his little gamble. But I am tolerable anxious over the important matter of hiking along home to milk the cows. I'm going to pass out that door and I'd hate to hustle any of you fellows unnecessarily."

He took a step toward them. There was an involuntary movement to retreat. Pullar laughed and the threshers, with wild yells, rushed at their prey. Above the clamour rose the bull-like roar of McClure.

"Throw the big stiff!" he shouted. "Mush him under

your boots before his gang get here. Put him out and we'll handle them."

With answering shouts they leaped to the attack. Pullar stepped back lightly, feigning retreat. Drawn by the ruse two sprang after him. Suddenly they felt a clutch like steel. Separating the two assailants he brought them together with a trap-like shutting of his muscular arms. Their heads met with a muffled shock and he sent them reeling to the wall. Hands were grasping for him as he shot out his right fist and his left and two more of his demented foes sank to their knees. Making a lightning side step he sprang away, freeing himself from the gripping tentacles of the gang.

In a flashing glimpse he found that he had dodged the attack en masse only to throw himself in the path of Snoopy Bill Baird. The huge slouching form was charging him wickedly. He twisted aside to elude the onset but was unable to avoid the kick of the heavy boot. It caught him along the cheek-bone, ripping the flesh. He closed, clinching his assailant. The big fellows were well matched, but with a confusing speed Pullar had pinned Baird's arms in a girdling grip. Tripping his great, writhing captive over his hip he flung him clean away above his head. Like a flying missile the man shot through the air, crashing down sprawlingly upon a pool table.

Pullar was not aware that his huge antagonist lay on the table a groaning heap, for they were dragging him down on all sides. Two of his assailants clung to his arms, robbing him of any means of defense, while a third belaboured him fiercely about the head. Still another fastened on his throat. This latter clutched Pullar's neck with both hands, gouging his thumbs into the windpipe with vicious design to strangle. The vital grip began to tell

10

and slowly at first, then with a chuck, they went to the floor.

"Hold him! Hold him!" shouted McClure gleefully as he danced about seeking a chance to strike. But a sudden change came over the battle. The fall had shaken the bulldog clutch. By a prodigious effort Pullar wrenched his right arm free. There was a series of quick, jabbing motions and the four assailants fell magically away. With a bound Pullar was on his feet facing McClure. The latter struck furiously for the face but his blow was swept aside by something rigid. Pullar stood inside his enemy's guard. He had but to strike and it would be over. He did not strike. Instead he smiled through the blood and stepped lightly back.

"No, McClure!" said he with a grim smile. "I don't need to."

The other looked at him a moment then breathed a low oath of surprise. At that instant there was a great shout and the Valley Gang charged through the door. Turning to the gang Ned Pullar lifted his hands and shouted out above the tumult:

"Back, men! This fracas is over!"

"Not on yer life!" cried Easy Murphy, angered to fighting-mad pitch by the sight of the bloody face of his boss.

"The fight is over!" cried Ned, holding back his men.

"Begobs! Ye don't know this wan Irish divil, Ned?" screamed Murphy. "I wull be afthurr pluggin' the lights uv me frind McClure."

At the words he stepped toward McClure, followed by the others. But he was intercepted by a swift motion of Pullar.

"No, Easy!" cried the young boss firmly. "Stick with me,

lad. This is my powwow. We are about to smoke the pipe of peace."

For a fleeting instant he caught the Irishman's eye. The flash of intelligence that passed between them checked the belligerent passion in Murphy's wild heart. With a significant and rueful nod the thresher agreed to Pullar's wish.

"Ah, Ned, darlint!" said he affectionately, taking in the room at a sweeping glance. "For why have ye bin mussin' up Rob's bowld byes? 'Tis a cyclone blower ye are, me hearty. Go ahead wid the show. The Valley Gang's occupyin' the front sates."

With a very bad grace the Valley Outfit followed their spokesman's lead. The eyes of the two gangs turned to Ned.

Aside from the gash along his cheek he was unhurt. Walking in among McClure's men he picked up his pipe. Repacking the tobacco carefully he lit up. Throwing a series of blue circles to the ceiling he indulged in a moment's reminiscence. Finally he spoke, addressing Easy Murphy in his usual quiet tone.

"A few minutes ago," said he, "Rob McClure was eating his head off over a certain little proposition when—we had a slight interruption. In fact, I was anxious to get home to the milking. I have changed my mind. Rob's proposal will interest you. He wants to stack his huskies up against the Valley Gang on a thirty-day run. He contends laying down a trifle of five hundred dollars that he can lick my gang——"

Here arose a sudden commotion, savage threats and a sinister movement of the Valley Gang. Ned waved his men back with a laugh.

"Just a minute, lads," said he. "Let me have my say. McClure pretends that he can lick the Valley Outfit in a thirty day out-put. Strange as it may seem I cannot agree with him. If he will make a real bet, make it cash and approve Jack Butte as holder of stakes, we'll be able to start something right off the bat."

On the heels of his words rose a chorus of defies from his men. Hands flew to pockets and wads appeared. Snoopy Bill caught his feet groggily scenting a gamble. In Rob McClure's eyes shone the gleam of the shark.

"Now you're spunking up!" said he with a sneer. "Butte's our man."

Turning to one of his gang, he said:

"Scoot out, Ford, and get him."

While the man started off to carry out his bidding he whipped out his check book and filled in a form. As Snoopy Bill spied the amount he let out a low whistle.

"Two thousand!" he exclaimed. "Rob, you're a la-la."

McClure handed the book to Pullar. Ned read it with immobile face. Amid a deep silence the crowd pressed around the bosses. Would Pullar call the bluff?

The year of which we write was the fall of nineteen hundred. The smoke of the tractor was rarely seen in the land. Of the gas-power machine there was no sign whatever. For five years Ned had swung steadily along the Valley's brow with his twenty-horse, thirty-six inch portable mill, threshing the line of farmers rimming the northern bank of The Qu'Appelle. If a farmer got Pullar's mill it assured him a straight crew, a quick, clean job and all his grain. The Valley Gang was thoroughly workmanlike, the crack outfit of the Pellawa stretches.

This supremacy was now disputed. Some ten years before McClure had come from the East with bags of money and bushels of confidence, not to mention a stock of real

13

ability. He was keen to get and heady and aggressive in the getting. Three years before he had entered the threshing game and pitched in with his usual gusto. One of his first moves was to cross the Valley and make a bold raid on Pullar's run. But his effort failed. Pullar's line of jobs remained intact. He managed to pick up a few farmers thrown on the threshing market through the defunct condition of their syndicate machine. Since Pullar's outfit was full up for a big season the cluster of jobs fell to McClure. The farmers of the Pullar run threw out some banter and an occasional jab resenting the attempt of McClure to cut in. This nettled McClure and was the small beginning of a bitter rivalry. Smothering his chagrin McClure set to work to build up a gang that would lower the colours of the Valley Outfit. At the end of the season it was found that Pullar's bushelage had far exceeded that of the rival machine. The following year repeated their fortunes. Then McClure startled Pellawa by exchanging his portable outfit for an immense forty-inch separator driven by a thirty-horse tractor steam power, of course. The new machine was equipped with self-feeder, self-bagger and cyclone blower. Adding extensively to his run he put on a large gang and began the season with everything in his favour.

Though facing alarming odds, Pullar took up the gauge in his quiet way. Rumours of record days by both machines drifted about the settlement with the result that the annual threshing derby began to show a tendency toward even money. The interested public pricked up its ears, enjoying the come-back of Ned. This popularity, with the complication of a three-day boose fest, was responsible for McClure's insulting challenge.

14

Ned was still scanning the check when Jack Butte appeared in the doorway.

"Just in time, Jack!" greeted Ned with a grin. "Hold this money for McClure. We are hooking up for a two-hand game, gang for gang."

There was a roar of applause from the Valley threshers. Above the noise rose the voice of Easy Murphy. He was performing the sailor's hornpipe before the shifty form of Snoopy Bill.

"Come across wid yer dust," challenged Murphy. "Fifty till fifty we skin ye aloive!"

"Taken!" was the eager acceptance. "Here, Butte's the dough. You can hand it back when the cows come home."

Butte was deluged with wagers.

"Hold your horses!" cried he, lifting protesting hands. "Two at a time. Come along quietly and we'll fix it all snug."

Taking out his note-book he made punctilious entry of all stakes. His task completed he took the trouble to plainly restate conditions.

"I'll bank this bunch of grass," he concluded. "The game winds up at eight P.M. on the last day of October. We'll meet in Louie Swale's Emporium and cash in. Meet me there at ten o'clock. And, gentlemen — —"

He paused, reading the faces of the bosses and their men with keen eyes.

"This game's to be run on the square. Do you get me?"

"Right-o!" agreed McClure. "We'll shear these lambs on Hallowe'en."

Ignoring the jibe Ned Pullar pointed to the checks wedged in the pile of bills. They were McClure's and his own. Speaking quietly to Butte he said:

"You'll cash those papers and re-bank the whole

15

amount in your own name?"

"Exactly!" replied Butte, flashing sharp eyes at the young boss.

"Good!" was the low response.

Taking a step nearer McClure, Pullar fastened his eyes on the face of his enemy. The lips of the older man were parted about to make some insulting fling when he bit his tongue. Ned's eyes were smiling but behind the smile glittered an ominous light that made McClure strike an attitude of defense. He retreated a step, watching the other. In an instant the air was electric. There was a shout from the Valley men and they leaped up beside their boss.

"Since this little deal is satisfactorily arranged, McClure," said Ned casually, "it may occur to you that your cows need milking. At any rate, the Valley Gang have taken a sudden whim to be alone. Think it over. We'll give you exactly one minute to get out. If you are here sixty seconds hence we'll maul you a little and—throw you out."

Ned took his watch from his pocket while the Valley Gang let out a defiant and joyful shout.

There was a malignant growl from the belligerent gang across the room at the sudden challenge. Rage swept over them but they made no move to close with their taunting enemies. The Valley men flung jeer and jibe in wild effort to provoke a charge. Hissing a terrible oath McClure turned to his men. What he saw decided him. Pointing to the door he addressed them.

"Cowards!" he snarled. "Get out!"

With a slouching alacrity they obeyed, vanishing through the door in swift and ignominious retreat. McClure passed after them without a word.

"Tin seconds till spare, the lucky divils!" cried Easy

16

Murphy regretfully.

At his rueful words the Valley Outfit lifted a victorious roar, following McClure and his men with shouts of derision.

Ten minutes later as Ned Pullar stood in the pool-room door a white horse dashed by, cantering along the slushy street. Astride swayed the form of a girl clothed in a slicker. Beneath her quaint hood flashed the light of brown eyes. Their quick glance caught his salute. She acknowledged the greeting by a dainty tip of her head and the faintest of smiles.

The slight recognition sent his blood atingle. In a moment she disappeared about a building. The vision of the girl remained with him and a shadow contended with the pleasure the sudden meeting had brought into his face. Finally the shadow triumphed and a deeply troubled look came into his eyes.

"Ah, Mary!" he reflected. "Where will this day's work lead us?"

The girl was Mary McClure, only child of his avowed enemy.

II

THE VALLEY OF GOLD

The wind drifted along the valley crisp with the breath of the harvest dawn. It blew gently over the prairies flowing in from the west. Speeding valleyward a horse and rider zigzagged in easy canter through the shrublands. They

17

clung to the deep paths of the buffaloes, dug long years ago by countless droves threading their way to the stream in the great ravine.

It was the girl's delight to "trail" these grass-grown ruts through the dense groves hanging shaggily to the south banks. In a little they ran out on a high shoulder of The Qu'Appelle. Here the bare hill was ribbed with the parallel paths to the number of seven or eight that slipped over the ravine crest, disappearing a few paces below into a thick grove of stunted oak. Halting the eager broncho, the girl let her eyes rest on the valley.

It was a pretty gulf cleaving the prairie for a width of two or three miles and winding out of sight into the blue distance. There was visible the shine of lakes and their linking streams. Under the amber light of the autumnal sunrise the valley was pricked out into a landscape of gold. The bank upon which they stood swept away to the southeast in a forest crescent wonderful with the variegated leafage of the searing year. Paling greens, bright yellows, faint oranges mingled with browns and buffs and the brilliant wines and reds. Falling away from their feet the colourful forest was a charming Joseph's coat, but in the spacious distance its mottled glory blent into the russet-yellow of the prairie autumn.

The north bank rose beyond, walling the ravine in a billowy rank of great, rounded hills bald as the skull of the golden eagle and seamed with dark lines of wooded gulches. Here and there along the crests hung over the edges of the great, harvest blanket, strips of wheat fields studded with their nuggets of brown stooks. In the blue radiance above drifted a fleet of soft clouds with creamy breasts and fringes of amber fire. On the floor of the valley lay a lake spread out in a broad silver ribbon that rose to the skyline for miles into the west.

"You beautiful Qu'Appelle!" cried the girl softly. "We love you—Bobs and I."

For many minutes she revelled in the ecstasy of gleaming morning and golden valley, her cheeks bitten to roses by the tanging wind-drift. At length she granted release to her impatient horse and let him dash down into the trees. Under their branches she drew him to a walk and, leaving the selection of their trail to the petulant Bobs, abandoned herself to the alchemy of the harvest woods.

Passing slowly through the depths of a grove of white-stemmed poplars they ran out into a tiny glade. Here The Willow, a pretty brook, dammed by industrious beavers, gathered itself into a little pond before its last wild rush to the lake. As they cleared the trees Bobs pricked up his ears and quickened his step, giving a low whinny. His rider glanced curiously ahead, surprised to see a horseman in the pool. Her face changed suddenly from surprise to pleasure. The horse was sipping the cool water. The rider was Ned Pullar.

"Mary!" he cried delightedly, sending his horse through the stream. "This is my lucky day. Darkey and I have been haunting Willow Glade for an hour past hoping just this, but never dreaming that you and Bobs would really show up."

"How did you know I was coming?" demanded the girl happily.

"I did not know," was the reply. "I only knew this to be one of your favourite haunts on a Sunday morning and conceived a long chance of meeting you here. It was necessary to have a personal talk with you. This morning I determined to see you before the day was gone."

"Are you in trouble, Ned?" cried the girl suddenly, a soberness driving the pleasure from her face.

"Very great trouble, Mary," said Ned. "Do you not know?"

Deeply he searched the eyes looking into his. He could tell by the innocence, the solicitude of them that they had not learned the thing he feared. He was greatly relieved.

"What is it, Ned?" was her anxious query. "I have heard of no trouble."

"Perhaps it is only a cloud over the sun," was the reply. "It may pass by. Indeed you have brightened things a lot for me already. Let us breathe our broncs while we talk it all over."

Slipping from his saddle he assisted her to dismount. Taking charge of the horses he secured them to adjacent trees and followed to where she had seated herself on a gnarled log at the foot of the little falls.

"I have a little surprise for you," said he, throwing himself on the leaves at her feet. "I am not returning to college this fall."

Her eyes opened wide, expressing a mystified incredulity.

"Sad but true!" was his reiteration.

"But your year, Ned! It is your final. You must finish."

"Sheer foolishness, eh? This smashing of a final year? So it seemed to me for a little. Only a little. I cannot leave Dad."

At the words he averted his eyes.

She studied the downcast face, an expression of pride growing in her eyes.

"You understand, I am sure," said he softly. "It has been worse this vacation than ever before. Dad's at a great disadvantage now and I have to watch him like a lynx. Swale's bar is a powerful lodestone. But he is bracing gamely. He has not touched the stuff for three weeks and if I stay with him now I believe he'll win out. Then I'll not lose the year after all. A steady grind at the homestead should work out an extra-mural pass, and I could pull down my degree with the rest of you."

"You will be missed, Ned."

He looked up quickly into her eyes. They were a peculiar mixture of sympathy and fun.

"Undoubtedly!" agreed Ned disconsolately, though his eyes twinkled. "How the Registrar will grieve at the non-appearance of my hitherto regular fee. And Grimes, sweet janitor! He will drop not a tear, but a diabolic wink at my sudden demise."

"Mercenary Registrar!" sighed Mary. "And unspeakably happy Grimes! Doubtful mourners, I admit. But others will follow the two chiefs. I see the Rugby Team pacing after slowly and aghast. They mourn Captain and star punter at one fell stroke or rather in the unavailable person of one fellow, Pullar. Methinks there was to have been a great International Debate. But now?—How can I go on down the long line? Behold the Winged Seven, favourites for the Hockey Cup, now, alas, the Wingless Six! And the Eight-oared Crew?—Can you not see that you will be missed ever so little?"

Ned looked up with a rueful grin.

"Grave losses all," replied Ned. "The ironic heartlessness of the small Co-ed notwithstanding. Varsity will gradually recover from her terrible handicap. Infinitely more terrible is it for me. Calculate the unmaterialized wisdom of four hundred priceless lectures. But, after all—it is nothing."

21

"No-o?" commented Mary slyly in sceptical demur.

Ned glanced into the brown eyes in time to surprise a smile uniquely pleasing in its whimsical delight. Instantly they became mockingly sober.

"Mary!" said he seriously, holding her gaze. "Will you miss me?"

The girl's eyes wandered suddenly to tree, sky, brook, finally resting on a log at their feet.

"What a sudden switch from general to particular," said she, absorbed apparently in the task of pecking a hole in the bark with the dainty toe of her riding-boot.

Laughing quietly Ned proceeded.

"If you could peep into my mind, Mary, you would find a seething resentment there. And all because of you. Soon you will be rejoining the old class. There's the rub. I cannot conceive of Pellawa without you."

"Indeed?"

"And a very big 'indeed,'" aggrieved Ned. "To think that Rooter Combes and his rah-rahs will be in clover. This obsession has been actively depressing since last Thursday. Perhaps you remember riding by Sparrow's. You looked quaintly desirable in that chic, brown slicker——"

"With my face all spattered and Bobs a mud tramp!"

"I did not see Bobs at all, just a chicily hooded girl with peeping curls of brown hair, flashing eyes and a nod adorably imperious but very welcome."

"I should not have recognized you."

"But you did and at that particular moment the act was doubly precious to me. How can I resign you, Mary, to the too tender solicitude of Combes and those dear fellows?"

Mary tipped her head reflectively while she read his half-serious eyes.

22

"Is this your trouble, Ned?" said she smiling frankly down at him. "Do you mean that you will miss me—quite a little?"

"Just so. Since you comprise the population of Pellawa —for me. But——"

"You may not be called upon to forego the society of this so immensely necessary person."

Now it was his eyes that opened wide.

"I have a piece of big news for you," continued Mary, shaking her head wisely while she enjoyed his surprise. "I, too, am dropping out. No Varsity for me this term. You see me to-day, Ned, a specially permitted schoolma'am. Last Thursday as I rode by Sparrow's I was on my way to sign the entangling documents. Bridges are all burned. To-morrow I begin teaching—where do you think?"

He shook his head.

"In the school of—The Craggs. I shall be your very close neighbour. Mary McClure is not flitting away from you. Combes and his tender-hearted fellows should worry very considerably, I fancy."

"Mary, Mary!" was the elated cry. "I am sorry for you but riotously happy for myself."

She looked down upon him a moment with eyes brimmingly glad, then a shadow crept into them.

"I am spending this year with Mother and Dad," she said simply.

Looking earnestly at her he caught the shine of tears. Stifling the gay words leaping to his lips he rose and stepping to her drew her head to his breast.

"Mary," said he gently, "our work is planned for a year ahead. Home is the only place for us just now."

"We'll make it a great year, Ned," was the hopeful reply.

"When I was a little girl, everything good for Mother and Dad was described as 'bestest.' This is to be the 'bestest' year for our loved ones that they have ever known. Can we make it so?"

"You are only a little girl yet," said Ned, kissing the face turned up to him. "And this is to be their 'bestest' year. We shall see to that. Now for my trouble, the thing that drove me out to find you. These last moments have made it deepen rather than vanish. On Thursday afternoon, a short time before I saw you, I had an adventure. Have you heard of it?"

"Not even a rumour, Ned. Mother and I are not as intimate with Pellawa life as we should be."

"I am glad you have not heard," said Ned earnestly. "There was an encounter in the pool-room. Your father was involved."

At Ned's words a fear flashed into the girl's eyes.

"Your father and I have made rather slow progress in our mutual acquaintanceship. We got to know each other much better at Sparrow's. I cannot say the event has helped any. We are now enemies publicly acknowledged. At least your father so considers me. The clash was sharp and promises serious trouble ahead for us. It will hamper us not a little in our plans of the last few minutes."

"Ned!" she cried with lips a-tremble. "You did not fight? Not that?"

He looked at her, deeply troubled by the white face and the pain in her glance. She was looking at the scar on his cheek. He thought of the wager. A staggering regret swept over him. He was about to tell her the whole story, but now? No. She should not know all—just yet. Forcing a reassuring smile he replied:

"No. We did not fight. It was a touch and go but

24

resulted in nothing more than a sharp brush with your father's gang. That scratch is from the boot of Bill Baird. I was able to restrain the Valley Gang, thanks to Easy Murphy's loyalty. Otherwise the worst would have happened. We did not fight and I am confident I can give you my promise that we never shall."

Immense relief filled the girl's eyes.

"You were in a hard place," said she, her look of strange comprehension searching his face. "You held your hand because—because of our love. I know it."

Her sure intuition astonished him, but before he could speak she continued:

"There is startling cause for cheer in all this, Ned. If you can prevent the terrible possibility I am thinking of, you can win Dad."

"How would you have me do it, Mary?" was his abrupt appeal.

She pondered deeply, her eyes growing in solicitude as the moments passed. At length she looked at him with troubled face, shaking her head.

"I do not know," was her helpless confession. "How would you win him?"

"The only way is to play the man with him," was the slow answer. "He would turn over heaven or hell to break me. Obviously I must break him."

The girl shuddered at the words. Watching the quivering face he was surprised to hear her say:

"I know there is no other way. One of you must conquer. But there is a condition I want to make. You will be right, always, Ned, as well as irresistible. I know you will."

"I shall always have the right with me. I have it now,"

was the quick reply. "I expect to butt into stone walls at times, but we shall win out. There is only one great, lurking dread. Sometimes I fear your father may strike at me through you, we mean so much to each other."

As he spoke he fancied he saw in her eyes the glimmer of a haunting fear. But it vanished so swiftly he doubted he had ever glimpsed it. The big eyes reading his were heavy with grief. With sudden impulse he crushed her in the shelter of his great arms.

"I should not have breathed the thought," said he penitently. "Nothing conceivable can ever strike our love, Mary. You are not afraid?"

"Not of that," was the reply as she nestled contentedly within the strength of him. "Many things may happen, but not that. Just now Father is obsessed with his new friendship. It is a thousand pities that the friend should be Chesley Sykes. His presence in Pellawa is an ominous mystery to me. So far he has deported himself with desirable aloofness. May he continue to do so. He is completely outside of this beautiful moment. Let us forget him."

"And ride away together," suggested Ned.

"I have an hour yet," calculated Mary.

"We'll spend it riding No-trail Gulch," tempted Ned.

"Let us away," laughed the girl gaily. "For the trail— —"

"Is luring," completed Ned, leading her to the horses.

A moment later they clattered over the gravel bed of the brook and into the trees.

III
BOUQUETS

The month of October sped swiftly away in one long attack on oceans of stooks amid the blue blaze of cloudless skies. The threshers were having a run of "great weather" as the blank fields and the piles of straw averred. The matter of the McClure-Pullar wager had of course leaked out and become the one thrilling feature of the annual wind-up. Aside from the two gangs there was a keenly interested and, alas, gaming public. The sympathy of the plains went to Ned Pullar; the odds to Rob McClure. Jack Butte had become an inhuman sphinx. Into Jack's elevator had come the steady stream of grain from the contending mills but to no one had he divulged the respective records. No system of tapping his books had yet succeeded. This was due to the fact that Jack Butte was an irreproachable and resourceful stakeholder. As rare evidence of his unique qualifications he had sworn the secrecy of every farmer threshed by the rivals. It was a tribute to the sporting public that with but three days to run only one man knew of the interesting situation.

The Valley Outfit was resting. Ned Pullar was oiling-up and cleaning his engine during the dinner interim. Every bit of brass about her was gleaming gold while the friction surfaces shone clean like new silver. The "Old Lady" had established a personal reputation in the Valley as a "mighty good engine," and her engineer was justly proud of her. To Ned she had become a living thing. Mounting on the footboard he grasped the throttle. During the pounding grind of the past month he had formed the habit of communing with this thing of power that he controlled with so masterful a hand. As his eyes read gauge and water-glass with satisfaction he spoke to the engine, addressing her not by word of mouth but with the voice of his reflection.

"Just a couple of days more and we'll ease up on you, old girl. You've been a game old Pal and you'll not throw me down now."

The Old Lady made violent protest at even the hint of such infidelity by throwing a hissing cloud of steam from her exhaust. Ned smiled, gripping the throttle with a fond clutch.

"Same old ready bird!" said he. "Eager to get at it, are you? Just five minutes, Old Lady, and we'll set you purring again."

With the flames roaring through her flues the thing of steel waited restively for the thing of will that held her levers in sinewy grasp.

At the separator the men resting for a few minutes upon the straw were looking up into the face of Andy Bissett, the separator man, listening to him as he worked away with wire prod and oil can.

"I tell you, lads, we are up against a stiffer proposition than any of you fellows think. Ned's out for blood. He doesn't care a whiff for that wager Butte holds. But he's got to win it."

"Hold on, Andy!" cried Lawrie, the big feeder. "You've got me up in the air. I thought the Valley Outfit was after McClure's long green."

"So they be," agreed Dad Blackford belligerently. "And

Ned, 'e's a-goin' to get hit."

But Andy shook his head.

"You don't get me," said he, pausing in his work. "And I can't explain for I'm as much at sea as the rest of you. But we've got to win this little bet. If we put it over McClure it will only be by a thousand or two. Ned says he won't push the Outfit any harder, but I've taken the liberty to put on the squeeze play for a couple of days. Grant's putting on two extra stook wagons and a couple of men. Here they come now. We're going to slam through a couple of thousand above the regular. If Grant can bung this old fanning mill I don't know it."

The men leaped to their feet, for the extra wagons had rattled up. There was a fresh determination in every face. They had been working at high pressure for the long run, but they were right on their toes in the face of the challenge. Each man went to his place addressing himself to the struggle in the workmanlike fashion of the Valley Outfit. Jean Benoit, the little French bagger, plucked the tankman's sleeve as the group broke up.

"What Ned hole on hees cheek?" questioned the Frenchman excitedly.

Easy Murphy looked at him a moment deeply puzzled. Suddenly light broke.

"Begobs, 'tis the tongue in his chake yer dappy about. Why, sez you, does not the sly divil be afthur-r showin' the hand uv him? Shure Ned's not wearin' his heart on his lapel, me frind from Montmorenci."

Jean searched the Irishman's face as it went through the contortion of an excessively wise and secretive wink.

"Mon Gar!" exclaimed the confused fellow. "De boss wan woodhead! Why he de debble not squeal? Eef we know, den lak wan blankety busy bee we work de whole gang. Eef we not know, Ned he ged him on de neck."

"You're right, Jean!" was the emphatic pronouncement. "And yit Ned wull not be afthurr tellin' his saycrits till the gintle lugs uv the Valley Gang. Can't ye see whut's eggin' him on? 'Tis not the wee wager. 'Tis a man." Tapping the Frenchman wisely on the breast he whispered tragically, "The boss is thrailin' a varmit be the cognomin uv Robbie McClure and he'll be afthurr gittin' his man dead or aloive. Put that intill the poipe uv ye and smoke ut, not forgettin' till wur-rk like — — in the manetoime. Farewell!"

Jean did not understand quite all but he turned to the bagger with fierce resolution. As he knocked the filling bag with his knee he caught sight of McClure's smoke through the cloud of dust enveloping him. His dark eyes shone.

"We lick heem! We lick heem!" was his low soliloquy. Then he added joyously as he gave the bag a vicious jab, "Ha! Eet will be good!"

The thought energized him mightily. Deftly settling the bag and closing it he seized it adroitly and by united force of arms, knees and back hurled it up into the wagon, remarking ferociously:

"So we give McClure the beeg fall. We give him beeg scare too, eh? And mebbe leetle licking also."

Smiling gleefully he settled to the grind.

Easy Murphy was absorbed in a brown study as he climbed up on his water tank and started his horses over the stubble. Suddenly he came out of the maze of his cogitations and called fiercely at his horses.

"Arrah, me beauties, shake the legs uv ye or I'll be afthurr pokin' yer rumps wid me number tins."

The horses took the hint and broke into a lumbering

trot. They were making a trip to the water-hole and at the moment were passing through a field of oats into which they would soon be hauling the Outfit. As he drove through the wire gate out into the road-allowance he saw a buckboard pull up at the fence some distance away. The sole occupant dropped out of the vehicle and passing through the strands of wire walked for a considerable distance into the stocks. Pausing for a moment the stranger knelt down beside a stock, then rising walked on to another, where he knelt again. His actions excited a keen curiosity in his observer.

"Begobs, me hearty!" exclaimed Easy. "Ye're not pickin' pansies in an oat-field. Nathur are ye adorin' the Almighty, for ye're almighty loike Snoopy Bill Baird, head foozler of McClure's bums. I'll hail yuh, Bill, till I find out yer tack."

He was about to yell when he checked himself, muttering:

"Howld yer jaw, ye owld fool."

The other had noticed his approach and loitered a few minutes shelling the grain, interested evidently in the yield. This matter duly settled, he climbed back through the fence and reëntering the buckboard drove slowly along toward the tank. It was Snoopy Bill all right. As they drew abreast Easy pulled up his horses. A roguish twinkle played in his eyes as he said:

"'Tis a foine day wur-r havin', Bill. A pleasant day indade for pluckin' swate bokays."

"Great day! Great day! Murphy!" was the jocular reply,

"Bin pickin' pansies the day," continued Easy naïvely, curious to discover what he could.

Snoopy Bill looked at him sharply. But no guile could he discover in the face grinning down at him.

"No such luck, Murphy," said he casually. "I was taking a squint at the yield. Pretty durn good, eh?"

"And it's the yield ye're afthurr meddlin' with and not the swate and gowlden daisies. I saw yuh pokin' around among the stooks as I pulled through the gate."

The smile on Snoopy Bill's face ceased to deepen while the whole man became suddenly alert. Easy Murphy caught the change.

"Ye're Snoopy Bill, shure enough," blurted he. "And I'll lay ye a tin-spot ye were up to no godly devowshuns kneeling in the muck by the stooks. Ye're not prominint for religion, are ye, Snoopy?"

Snoopy Bill's tone was galling to Easy's inflammable spirit as he replied imperturbably:

"Leaving the matter of the 'swate daisies' aside, Murphy. I was praying for you, honest. I was putting in a lick for the Valley Gang asking the good Lord to have a look to Pullar's Outfit when we clean them up."

Easy's jaw set, a sign that an ultimatum was imminent.

"Ye blatherin' spalpeen!" he cried, his hands opening and shutting convulsively. "I'll be afthurr spilin' yer sassy mug if ye open it agin."

Snoopy Bill opened his "mug" with commendable lack of hesitation. An impudent drawl pointedly accentuated did not tend to reduce Easy's evident irritation.

"Talking about mugs, Murphy," said he confidentially, "it seems to me we have some curious and fine large samples hereabouts gopping wide open for free inspection."

The sardonic grin that accompanied the casual observation touched off a whole magazine of high explosive. Easy's mouth was a generously ample specimen and his posture of attention was to sit with it ajar. The amplitude of

32

that particular area of his facial map was a source of constant regret. Hence the remark rankled.

"Ye've said it!" was his angry utterance as he threw down the lines. With a leap he was off the tank. They dropped to the road together, but Snoopy Bill having a shorter descent recovered first and rushing at his antagonist swung swiftly and struck, planting a powerful blow on the chest, hurling the other against the tank. He followed quickly for the head with his other hand but Easy's native wit acted with surprising speed and he ducked. Snoopy Bill's closed fist rapped on the hard surface of the tank, skinning the knuckles.

"Thry agin!" yelled the Irishman mockingly, with a vicious thrust into his enemy's ribs. The blow staggered his opponent. Swiftly he followed it with a jolting up-cut, yelling again, "Take wan yersilf and be hanged!"

The blow made Snoopy Bill's head bob back and he dropped to his knees. Easy stood over him furiously triumphant. Stooping he called into the other's ear:

"Git busy at yer devowshuns, me hearty. Put in a wur-rd for McClure and his divils."

With a weak smile Snoopy Bill staggered to his feet.

"You are a hard hitter, Murphy," said he dazedly.

Picking his late antagonist up bodily Easy bundled him into his buckboard and slapping the horse smartly on the hip sent him off at a trot. Placing his hands to his mouth the tankman shouted:

"If ye want anny more forgitmenots come back the morrow, the garden's full."

With this parting shot he climbed up on his tank and resumed his trip to the water-hole.

IV

THE MAN, ROB McCLURE

Rob McClure sat before his roll-top desk, his head resting
upon his hands. He was perturbed. Occasionally his head
would sink into a posture of dejection. In a moment he
would straighten, shrug his shoulders and look out of the
window, his face swept by the irony of an uncouth smile.

He was a man of powerful physique, large of frame,
possessor of a presence singularly impressive. He was
conscious of his power. An habitual, impatient shrug
revealed a restive spirit deeply antagonistic to baffling
elements. A relentless, implacable expression inwrought the
face that exhibited even in the act of smiling the dominance
of an over-riding will. There was something cruel in the
hard lines about the mouth, while the deep little wrinkles
about the eyes more than hinted brutal cunning. One felt
that given sufficient pressure Rob McClure was capable of
the unspeakable. There were, however, relieving features to
the hard visage, most prominent of all a high, expansive
brow and great, volcanic eyes.

Looking out of the window his eyes fell on the yellow
stretches of stubble, empty now save for the huge piles of
straw thrown up by the blower. In the west the plain was
gulfed by the blue depths of The Qu'Appelle Valley. His
glance swept over the autumn landscape all unseeing, for
his gaze was fixed on two streams of distant smoke that rose
for a little in straight columns, then floated off in long
parallel lines to the west. Clenching his fist he brought it

down on the desk.

"I've got him nailed!" he breathed fiercely, smiling his strange smile.

Then his confidence seemed to shake. The two lines of smoke were streaming over the fields evenly abreast.

"Pullar's a silent devil," he whispered darkly. "He is deep —deep as ——, and he cleans up a pile of stuff."

He meditated for a little then added decisively:

"But I've got him nailed tight."

The irresolution disappeared and the cruel smile stole out again.

"If he should win," was the jocular reflection. "We'll take a look at the little game proposed by Reddy Sykes. Reddy has a way—a fetching way." The name brought a certain merriness to his face. The humour was not attractive.

With a satisfied shrug he rocked back in his chair. As he did so his eyes rested on a photograph above his desk. Down upon him gazed two beautiful faces. Instantly a tender light softened the hard features. His lips moved, shaping involuntarily the names:

"Helen! Mary!"

The picture held his searching gaze until the sound of approaching footsteps broke the spell. At the sound the tender light vanished and a conflict surged over his face. Gradually his jaw set and the steel of the unyielding will revealed itself. The door opened quietly and in a moment a hand rested gently on his head. The voice that fell on his ear was sympathetic and affectionate. Mary had broken into his sanctum.

"Why, Daddy," she cried, "you are looking very serious. Are you troubled about something?"

The very solicitude of the voice seemed to chafe him.

"No," he exclaimed abruptly.

Nothing daunted she fondled his hair.

"Is the mill not running well, Daddy?"

The appeal in the voice caused a relenting of his face but his tone was forbidding as he replied:

"Yes. She's running along fine. I must go out to her right away."

Submitting brusquely to her kiss he rose and snapping the roll-top shut took his departure.

Mary McClure sat down in the vacated chair, resting her head on her hands as her father had done.

"Poor Daddy!" she murmured. "You are so busy, so preoccupied."

There was a trace of pain in the voice, a great wistfulness in the eyes. Once again she was confronted with the tragedy of affection unrequited.

Looking at the father one would expect in his daughter the robust, ample type. But she was small and fragile, a delicate bloom of young womanhood. Out of the bright face looked lustrous brown eyes, a seriousness lying in their playful depths. In appearance only was she fragile, for the small form was well compacted, lithe and wiry, capable of really great endurance. She was more than equal to exhausting rides along the ravine and the trails of the upper country. Sitting by the desk she was a diminutive, disconsolate figure. She had drooped into a pensiveness that of late visited her all too frequently. Nose and chin had the dainty grace of the spirituelle and such was Mary McClure. Yet was she human, fired with an intense passion for people. A quick, light glance of her eyes or the flash of her smile threw the spell that was irresistible. Life opened to her on all sides. The girl was fortunate in her mother. The glory of a

36

great affection enveloped her. In the mother appeared the culture of Old Varsity, giving to the McClure home a distinguishing atmosphere not often found on a Western farm. Helen McClure was a fine companion for the vivacious girl, and the two enjoyed a delightful camaraderie.

In her father Mary was presented with the most cruel enigma. Here lay the secret of the solemnness that so often filled her eyes. By him all affectionate approach was resented. He seemed deliberately striving to quench her natural attachment. But Mary's affection knew no repulse. Patiently she pressed the attack, intent on destroying the barrier he would insist on building between them. At times she fancied a relenting had rewarded her efforts.

Rising, she walked to the window and looked out pensively upon the autumn fields. Her heart was conscious of a dearth as great as that of the barren stubble. Her lips trembled as she whispered musingly:

"Daddy doesn't seem to want my love. Why is he so busy—so—so unfriendly? So buried from us in a hundred cares?"

As she pondered she shuddered, for she remembered times when he was well-nigh brutal. Then the fetid odour flowed from his breath. Rapt in the poignant moment her face drew into sad lines and a mist stole over her eyes, blurring the autumn vision.

McClure had made all haste and drew near his machine. As he approached the engine slowed up and stopped and the pitchers, jabbing their forks into the sheaves, lay down on the loads. Urging his horse to great speed he rode up to the machine. A lively altercation was in progress. A knot of excited men were gathered about Snoopy Bill Baird and Sid Smithers, the farmer. Smithers' voice rose high in angry tones.

"She stops right now," he cried vehemently. "And you pull your Outfit off my farm."

Throwing down the lines McClure strode in among the men. His heavy voice rose above the hubbub.

"What's the kick?" was his demand.

"Smithers is trying to put a crimp in this job," replied Snoopy Bill. "He's ordered the mill off the farm. He contends we're throwing over his grain."

Smithers interposed warmly.

"And you are doing it," said he wrathfully. "It's a cussed shame. I can prove it. Come back to the straw pile."

He promptly led the way and the crowd moved back quickly to the blower. Reaching into the straw pile Smithers drew out a coal shovel. His voice was indignant as he said:

"Here's what I caught in five minutes at the mouth of that blower."

The men crowded round. Cleaning the straws away he disclosed a layer of plump yellow grains covering the bottom of the shovel. As the sight met his eye McClure gave an involuntary start and his face grew dark. His voice was mollifying, however, when he spoke.

"That looks pretty bad, Smithers," said he quietly. "But you just happened to catch a shoal of grain thrown over on a bunch of straw. I'll bet you ten to one we haven't thrown over five bushels in the last three days."

But Smithers stood firm.

"You can't pull the wool here, McClure," was the menacing retort. "There is a heap of my stuff going over and you quit. Easy Murphy gave me a line on Grant's yield and he's beating me bad. My crop's as good as Grant's and you know it. Haul your Outfit off my farm."

Smithers was determined. For a moment McClure was silent. Then he spoke in an appeasing tone.

"I don't want to quit this job right now," said he. "I'll tell you what I'll do. Let me finish this run in my own way and if your yield doesn't equal Grant's I'll make up the shortage and not charge you a sou for your threshing. Is that square?"

Smithers turned the matter over deliberately.

"Make it law," said he shrewdly, "and I'll hook up with you."

"Agreed!" was the quick response. "I'll sign the papers to-night. Meet me at Reddy Sykes' at ten and we'll put it through."

"Go ahead on that condition," said Smithers, climbing into his wagon.

Quickly the men were in their places and the machine went roaring into the twilight. As McClure stood by the separator he signalled to Snoopy Bill.

"Let her rip, Bill," was his shout. "Crowd through a couple of thousand extra before to-morrow night."

Snoopy Bill passed the word and the engineer opened the throttle. The gang responded with a will and soon a great stream of straw was gushing from the blower.

At that moment Mary McClure was standing up in her stirrups with eyes fixed intently on a spur of the north bank of the Valley. As she watched, a yodling scream came over the rounded hilltops. She smiled delightedly. On the tip of the lofty spur she caught sight of a red flash that she knew instantly as the shining coat of a certain bay broncho.

"It is Flash with Margaret up!" was the pleased

exclamation. "I believe she wants me."

Forming a horn with her hands she called back in the cry of the hills. The rider on the spur waved her gauntlet in reply, beckoning to the rider in the Valley. Instantly Mary turned Bobs into the trees, sending him up a steep bridle path to the left. In a few minutes the girls were together and they set out through the stubble to where the Valley Gang was finishing the wheat.

"We are just in time to see the move," said Margaret. "For you, of course, the engineer is the whole gang. You will be able to see Ned in action."

"And you will be absorbed in the rest of the gang, that is in the antics of the separator man," countered Mary.

"At present," laughed Margaret, "I am going to make a raid on your preserves and talk to Ned."

She rode up to the engine.

At that moment there was a boisterously gallant salute from the gang, accompanied by a vigorous waving of caps and the shrill scream of the engine. The girls acknowledged the reception by a gay flourish of gauntlets.

"We are going to time the move, Ned," shouted Margaret above the roar of the engine, showing him her watch. "Let us see what the Valley Outfit can do."

Drawing his watch from his pocket Ned blew the whistle, promptly gaining the attention of the whole gang. Waving his hand toward the site of the new setting, he lifted high his watch and pointed to Margaret. With a ringing cheer they accepted the challenge and addressed themselves to the race against time. One of the feats of a crack outfit is the swift move to a new setting without mishap or confusion.

Already the last stock teams have pulled away from the

separator and are careering in wild race to the adjacent field. With the tossing in of the final shovelful of chaff the separator stands clean and naked above the stubble. As the last bit of wheat dribbles into the bag Ned signals the stop and Margaret lifts her watch aloft.

"It is up to the Valley crew now," comes the silvery challenge, and the boys respond with a merry shout and the address that marks the discipline of the gang.

As the fly-wheel slows up the pitchers deftly throw the belt, roll it up and hang it in place. At the same time the carriers are lowered and secured and the two waiting grain-teams hooked to the separator. Leaning well on the lines the drivers give the word. With a sharp gee and a steady pull they haul the mill up on the stubble and head in a curved line for the site of the new setting a quarter of a mile away. There a space has been already cleared and a circle of loaded stook-wagons is beginning to form, awaiting the arrival of the machine.

The feat par excellence of all the teaming about a threshing mill is that of pulling the engine out of the holes into which she has settled and over the intervening stubble. Usually two teams are detailed to this duty, but here the big tank team is sufficient. At the drop of the belt Easy Murphy hitched the grays. The two big beasts stand expectant. Seizing the lines Easy gives the inspiration of his invigorating brogue. Thrusting their great shoulders at the collars the team leans steadily forward. Straining with their mighty muscles they sink their toes deep into the turf. The traces stretch into tense, vibrating thongs. Hawing sharply the real pull commences. The mass begins to move. Swaying slightly as his horses' heads go down, Easy heartens them.

"Stiddy now, me beauties, and aisy ut is or the stubble

wull be afthurr ticklin' the bellies uv ye."

Suddenly the wheels rise out of the holes and the heavy mass rolls along.

"Aye, 'tis an aisy waltz fer yez, me bantams!" crows the tankman as the big team swings through the soft muck with the weighty Old Lady in tow. At precisely the same instant the separator has made its start. Glancing at her watch Margaret is surprised to observe that barely a minute has elapsed.

Arriving at the cleared area the separator, under the guidance of Andy Bissett, circles to the east, coming up to position in the teeth of the wind. The engine takes a curve to the west, swinging east to meet it. With the separator in place and blocked, every man springs to his task. Carriers are swung into proper elevation, feeder and band-cutter's stands dropped and the belt run out to the engine.

Ned stands on the rear of his engine with eye sighting along the fly-wheel. Now is the critical moment. An inch too much to right or left means the loss of minutes.

"Gee a little!" comes the crisp command. "Steady ahead! Let her swing to gee! Easy now! Hold!"

At the final order Easy Murphy brings his horses to a dead stop. Quickly the belt is slipped on and tautened. Every man stands in his place poised for work. Two short shrieks of the siren and the whole scene leaps into animation. Volumes of smoke belch from the funnel, the big belt speeds flapping along to the separator, starting the whirring of a maze of lesser belts and the spinning of countless pulleys. In a moment the cylinder is devouring an endless flood of sheaves. From the side of the mill the oats gush out while the straw rolls up over the carriers in a golden stream.

The girls ride up to the engine, admiration in their eyes.

"What time did we kill?" inquired Ned, smiling through his layers of grease.

"You made time," corrected Mary, flashing a bright smile down upon him. "That was wonderful work, quite worthy of the Valley Outfit."

"Time," said Margaret with official dignity, "is the surprising record of eight minutes and twenty seconds."

"I must let the gang know," said Ned in high elation. "That is a pretty decent record." Reaching out he blew eight screeching calls. The threshers paused long enough to respond with a trio of husky cheers. Then back they went with a will to the grind.

"What a furiously busy gang you have, Ned," was Mary's ingenuous observation, her eyes on the lively sight. "You all work as if we are to have a two-foot fall of snow, during the night. Why this haste?"

Ned smiled peculiarly and was silent. Margaret came quickly to his relief. She was aware of the exact situation and entirely disapproved, but she knew Ned wished to hold the truth from Mary.

"The Valley Outfit have been rushing along at this breakneck speed for the whole of October," said Margaret. "They are gambling, Mary. The boys have a wager that they can pile up a record output for the month. The trial winds up to-morrow night. Ned Pullar and his vaunted Valley Gang are a company of very foolish gentlemen."

"There are exceptions in the case, I suspect," insinuated Mary. "Our little Miss Grant exempts all tall, good-looking separator men. Hum!"

Ned laughed.

"Were it not for the dust," said he, "I would take you girls over for a chat with our rather handsome fellow. I have

43

a hunch, however, that Margaret would scarcely enjoy it."

"What? The handsome fellow?" posed Mary mischievously.

"No. The dust," replied Ned.

"It is a little matter," agreed Margaret.

"The handsome fellow?" teased Ned.

"No. The dust," prompted Mary archly.

All three laughed.

"Here, White!" called Ned to his fireman. "You handle the throttle while I take the girls to the mill."

In spite of the dust the four-cornered interview though necessarily brief resolved itself into a charming "little matter." Andy was back in his place on top of the mill oiling near the carriers. Ned stood beside the girls, who were sitting their horses just beyond the cloud of dust. They were enjoying a few moments' contemplation of the lively scene before departure for the Grant homestead when suddenly a vivid light flashed red in the twilight, flaring on the sweating face of Lawrie, the big feeder. Instantly followed a loud metallic crashing. With a strange, muffled shout Lawrie threw up his hands and fell on the feed table, pitching forward into the jaws of the machine. An instant more and he must be seized by the deadly teeth of the whizzing cylinder.

At the blare of fire Ned uttered a cry of alarm and rushed toward the separator. Realizing Lawrie's horrible plight he shouted to White at the throttle and taking a lightning leap drew himself up on the separator above the whirring teeth. Already they were fanning the hair of the insensible feeder as his head settled nearer to the blurred shine of the hideous jaws. Reaching over, Ned seized the helpless man and lifted him by the sheer strength of his powerful arms out of the fangs of the machine. But the weight of his inert burden swinging suddenly overbalanced him. Poised over that maw of whirling death the two men hung for an awful instant as Ned fought to recover. But the weight was too much; Lawrie began to sink. It was evident the two men were falling back into the cylinder. A scream of terror leaped from the lips of the horror-stricken band-cutters. Then it was Ned felt his shoulder clutched in a mighty grip and he with his precious burden was dragged back to the roof of the mill.

"Thank God you were there, Andy!" exclaimed the big fellow breathlessly as they composed the huddled form of the unconscious Lawrie.

"A touch and go, Ned!" was the solemn rejoinder. "I did not know anything was amiss—until I heard your shout. It took me an instant to spot you in the dust. Lawrie's badly smashed."

And so it seemed, for the man's face was washed with blood.

Meanwhile White had shut down and willing hands helped them move the wounded man to the ground. Water was speedily applied and the blood sopped up, revealing a deep gash along the forehead gouged by some missile thrown out by the rotating cylinder. Under the steady bathing there were soon signs of returning consciousness. Slowly opening his eyes Lawrie was surprised to find Ned bending over him, looking at him with anxious, sober gaze. A gleam of intelligence crept into the man's face and he smiled faintly.

"Oh, yes!" he said reminiscently. "I remember. I felt it slip in and tried to draw it back but it got away." After a moment's pause he added: "I am afraid it has played hob

45

with the cylinder and concave. Have you taken a look, Ned?"

"You Lawrie!" cried Ned, smiling at the game fellow. "It's the man first here, you know. How are you feeling?"

"O.K., Ned, though by gum I seem to have taken the count."

Recovering he rose on his elbow and looked around curiously. The gang were gathered about him, a circle of solemn faces. Giving a little laugh he said naïvely:

"What's got your goat, pals?"

"Shure 'tis the lucky, quare divil ye are," said Murphy, "till be dead wan minute and assistin' at your own post mortin the nixt."

A hearty laugh passed round the circle relieving the tension. No more was said, but Lawrie understood the grip of Ned's strong hand.

"We must fix that cut, Lawrie," said he, looking helplessly about. "This dirt will never do."

The moment the girls realized the accident they had dismounted and assumed the official duties of Red Cross first aid. Mary McClure smiled at Ned's words. She had already arrived at a solution. Rising from her place beside Lawrie she spoke.

"Ned," said she curiously, "have you a knife?"

"Here," was the prompt response as he produced a jack-knife.

"Margaret, you take it," said the girl, "and if the Valley Gang will close their eyes for a minute I'll direct you what to do."

At the words she lifted her skirt daintily, revealing the snowy white edge of the petticoat beneath. With dancing eyes the gang made the right about turn and Lawrie decided on an immediate snooze. A few minutes later his brow was bound with a clean bandage and he was making his way shakily to the feed-board. Calling a farewell the fair riders rode away over the stubble, followed by the applause of the grateful fellows.

Meanwhile at the machine there were interesting developments. Jean Benoit, who was working in on the shakers, gave a sudden shout and popped up out of the separator holding something in his hand. It was a heavy wrench. He examined it in a puzzled manner for a moment then handed it to Easy Murphy. The tool was minus one of its jaws. On the remaining jaw some initials had been punched, but they had been almost obliterated through the recent offices of a file.

"Dat no Valley wrench!" exclaimed Jean.

"Probably one of Grant's left on the stock during the binding," said Ned.

Easy Murphy shook his head sceptically.

"Ah!" was his fierce cry as he tipped the tool at a new angle to the light. "So I think. By the Howly St. Paddy! Take a look, Ned. Can you see?"

Ned took a look and there in the bright shine of the filed surface were good traces of the punch marks forming plainly the letters, R-M. Over him swept an ominous conviction. Without a word he placed the wrench carefully in the tool-box.

"'Tis the hand uv Snoopy Bill," said Easy Murphy darkly. "And 'tis his foul plot near did fer Lawrie and Ned." Clenching his hands he dropped suddenly into a vengeful silence.

A desire for revenge swept through the gang like an electric shock. Even Ned's cool eyes emitted a dangerous glare. Andy Bissett saw the dire change in his companion. Laying his hand on Ned's shoulder he said quietly:

"Ned, it's a dastardly trick but Lawrie will be well in half an hour. It's up to the Valley Outfit to call the bluff and play the winning card. Half a dozen teeth are gone in the concave and several others twisted. The cylinder is about as bad. With fast work it will mean only a two-hour stop. Let us finish strong."

"Very well!" agreed Ned. But his face did not resume its usual imperturbable demeanour.

There was no more threshing that night. Morning found them out an hour earlier, however, pounding grimly ahead, bent on recovering the lost time. As Ned stood at the throttle, a masterful shadow in the gray dawn, he thought over the adventure of the night before. It seemed to hold some sinister portent. Easy Murphy had in the meantime recounted to him the episode with Snoopy Bill Baird. Two more heavy tools had been discovered in one of the loads. Suddenly he became conscious of the malignant nature of the foe with whom he was striving. His jaw set tightly and a mighty resolution shot from his eyes. Unconsciously he opened the throttle and the power throbbed with a fresh leap along the great belt. As he did so a vision flitted unexpectedly before him. He saw Mary McClure standing amid the gang, her eyes alight with laughter while she held her skirt daintily lifted to disclose the snowy fabric for Lawrie's wound. Suddenly his face lost its seriousness and he laughed delightedly.

"Mary!" he cried softly.

Shutting off the throttle he curbed the engine in her impulse to race.

"I guess we have a bunch of pressure left, Old Lady,"

said he confidently, as he guided her into steadiness. The thing of power steamed on into the strenuous day while the thing of will threw down the challenge of youth.

V

AT THE WATER-HOLE

Easy Murphy shaded his eyes from the sun as he gazed eagerly over the prairie. After a prolonged look he remarked:

"Begobs, I belave he's coming!"

A further scanning of the landscape elicited a cry of satisfaction.

"Nick's headin' fer the howl all right," said he elatedly.

The Irishman was standing on the tank, his hand on the pump-handle. He had backed the grays into a pool fed by a small creek that here expanded into a miniature pond some dozen yards across. In Western threshing the tankman draws his water from the nearest hole or stream. For some days both Easy and Nick Ford, the McClure tankman, had been filling their tanks at the same pool.

Nick Ford was known familiarly as Boozey Ford, a self-explanatory sobriquet. Whiskey aside, he was one of the most reliable tankers along the Valley. With whiskey by his side his water-wagon was apt to receive a diluted attention.

As the days sped by the struggle between the two outfits became intense. The two tankmen were nearing the point of interpersonal complications in their heated conversations on the issue. Easy Murphy was feeling irrepressibly loquacious on this occasion, for he had not met

Boozey since the affair of the R-M wrench. However, as Nick drove up he began a foxy approach, greeting him in a friendly manner.

"Nick! How is the wur-r-rld using you?" was his opening.

"So, so!" was Nick's no less friendly response.

"Ye'll be afthurr faylin' a demi-semi-quaver in yer boots, Nick, since till-night's the night the Valley Outfit take the candy from the kid."

"There's sure going to be a lark to-night," agreed Nick. "We'll have a howling time putting the kibosh on your little, old Outfit. You mark my words, Murphy, when Jack Butte hands out his estimates you'll freeze stiff. I'll bet you even money we lick you by a thousand."

"Just cover that wee trifle," said Easy, revealing a ten-dollar bill.

"Sorry to rob you, Murphy," said Nick, "but it's awfully decent of you to accommodate me. We'll hand it to Butte just before the curtain goes up."

"'Tis a great pleasure till contribute," agreed Easy light-heartedly. Then he added slyly, "By the way, Nick, did ye miss anny tools from yer tool-chist lately?"

"Not that I know of," was the frank reply.

"Shure we found wan uv Rob McClure's wrenches in our separator yisturr-day."

Nick's interest perceptibly increased.

"'Tis not the act uv a gintleman, but a dirty trick uv Snoopy Bill Baird, and 'tis achin' I am till spile the impudint jaw of the Snoopy wan fer the same foul act."

Nick's blood began to sweep into his animated face. But the other continued:

"Howld yer timper, lad. I'm not afthurr blamin' you,

Nick. Yer as innocent as the lambs in the spring."

His voice grew sweet as honey and he made a suspicious motion to his breast pocket.

"We'll just have a wee dthrop as gintlemen together on the head uv the divilmint, and part—frinds."

He drew an amber-coloured flask from his pocket.

"'Tis the rale Irish, Nick. Be afthurr washin' down a swate swallow."

He extended the bottle convivially.

Nick took in the sight with fascinated and thirsty eyes. All hostility magically vanished and a supreme joy capered shamelessly into his face.

"Don't care if I do," said he, with a too casual unconcern. "Dad, that's prime stuff!" was his genuine approval as he handed back the flask.

"Shure I'm afthurr sayin' the same mesilf. Yer over modest, lad. Take a sip that wull tingle the toes uv ye."

So gracious a pressure was not to be resisted, and Nick responded with a ready acquiescence that left nothing to be desired. Easy emulated in pantomime, tipping the flask adroitly but permitting no drop to pass his lips. Taking another "sensation," Nick scurried off to his own tank and began pumping vigorously. Soon, however, he felt the desire for still another touch and was back at the flask. Easy Murphy kept the bottle supplied from some mysterious source about his person. So the best part of an hour passed and signs began to appear that Nick was rivalling the tanks in the quantity of liquid he was carrying. In the meantime Easy had leisurely filled his own tank. Suddenly The Mogul, McClure's giant engine, sounded the water call. Nick recognized the signal and, dropping the pump-handle, seized the lines and started off, urging his amazed horses in a line of patter that was new to them. As he drove away Easy slipped down off his own wagon and, stealing craftily after, tapped the bung of Nick's tank with a stone. One or two skillful knocks and the peg fell out, letting the water away in a heavy gush. Throwing the bung into the grass, Easy climbed up on his tank and followed.

Ahead drove Nick, supremely unconscious of the fact that his tank was fast emptying. When they reached the road-allowance he became suddenly confused. His trail lay directly across the road and into a field. His horses would have taken the right way, but Nick pulled them up sharply. His eyesight was temporarily impaired. He could see only the good road running east and west. Pulling on the left line, he turned into the east. Yet he was not sure, and drew up his horses once more. His tongue was thick as he called back:

"Hello, Eashy! (hic) Ish the trail (hic) all right?"

"Shure and indade it is that," came the wily response. "Go right ahead to yer outfit, Nick, man. It's a foine road, the smoothest in the howl counthry."

With a flourish of his whip Nick sent the unwilling team on down the road. Crossing the road-allowance, Easy entered the oat-field through the wire fence and made straight for his own machine. As he hit the stubble trail he heard the Mogul whistle impatiently for water. A moment later she called again. Turning around, he looked at Nick. He, too, had heard the urgent calls and was standing up driving like Jehu. The tank was now empty and the horses responded by breaking into a smart trot. The sight was hugely entertaining to the watcher. He slapped his thigh, shouting in unholy glee.

"Be the wake uv me grandmother!" he cried exultingly,

"it's now we get back the swate and precious minutes they filched by their rascalities uv yisterday."

Away in the distance Nick was driving like mad while the Mogul tattooed her calls for water with an angry insistence that drove him from her at accelerated speed. The circumstance was too much for the delighted Irishman. Laughing till the tears rolled down his cheeks he called after the disappearing Nick:

"Go it, me hearty! Kape it up, bye, and ye'll soon reach the broad Atlantic. Begobs! Call in at Winnipeg. They're shy on water-wagons in the Gateway uv the Gowlden Wist."

Never a word of the matter did he give to his young boss as he emptied his tank in preparation for the next trip. His wickedly radiant face attracted Ned, however, stirring his curiosity.

"What's tickling you, Easy? Been filling your boiler at Louie's tank?"

"Niver the dthrop, Ned. Not wanct since the twilfth uv July have I shined up till the dementin' crathur. 'Tis the whistle uv the Mogul that's drivin' me tipsy. Somehow the thirsty screamin' uv it tickles me since uv the rediculous."

"Rob's engine is out of water. She's been callin' for over half an hour," observed Ned, looking over the stubble at the rival outfit. "Indeed, Easy, she's hung up. Their blower is stopped."

At an unusual hearty chuckle from the tankman, Ned eyed him sharply, a suspicion leaping into his mind.

"Shtopped's the wurrd!" exclaimed Easy in feigned surprise, shading his eyes the better to study the Mogul. "Rob wull be afthurr havin' a brathin' spell. May it last a wake."

Ned's eyes detected an unusual excitement on his

companion's averted face. His suspicion took a sudden definite form.

"Easy," said he seriously, "you are mighty pleased about something and yet not at all surprised. Let me into the secret."

"Shure 'tis plazed I am this minute, Ned, and the most astonished critter on the Valley Gang."

"Steady, lad," cautioned Ned. "You can't fool me. You know more about the water shortage at Rob's outfit than Rob himself. What's keeping Nick?"

Easy found a matter for precipitate occupation in the barrel he was filling and did not reply at once. He was seized with sudden panic, for he had caught sight of Ned's face. The unsmiling eyes filled him with trepidation. When he at length looked up Ned's clear eyes looked through him. For once the garrulous Irishman was speechless while a blush flamed slowly over his brown face.

"Tell me," said Ned simply.

Hitching his overalls nervously and somewhat forcefully, Easy let a broad, sheepish grin play on his ample face. He attempted jocularity.

"'Tis a lugoobrius confession ye'll be draggin' out uv me wid the third degree uv yer blazin' eye."

"Tell me," repeated Ned.

"Wull," said Easy, scratching his head with obvious regret, "since 'tis implacabul ye are, I'll make it short and swate. Nick and yer humble sarvint meets at the mud puddle. We pass the complimints uv the sayson, git intill a small fracas uv the tongue and out uv it by the bottle. We had a wee dthrop. That is, Nick had. Thin he took another and another, et cetra and so on. Nick was oncommon thirsty. In a wurrd, I filled Nick till the neck and pulled the bung uv his tank. The one is impty and the other full. 'Tis the Mogul and mesilf knows which and,—yersilf, begobs, since ye tapped me wires. To sum up fer ye, me inquisitive frind, Rob's tank is impty and his tankman full, and the pair uv thim is headin' fer salt water at a spankin' trot. 'Tis comin' till the blackgards if ye ask Easy Murphy."

Easy stood before his boss with hanging head. His confession had not stimulated any risible emotions in Ned. Ned, on his part, said nothing, but stood looking for a little at the culprit, a kindly light mingling with the flash of his eyes. Then he stepped over to his engine and, seizing the whistle-cord, gave it a jerk, blowing the one sharp shriek that signals stop. Instantly the work ceased and the outfit slowed to rest. Amid the shouts of the men demanding the cause of the stop, Easy Murphy ran swiftly to Ned.

"Ye're not afthurr killin' the outfit," cried he, a peculiar pleading in his voice.

"Easy," said Ned quietly, "the Valley Outfit is running this little jig on the square. Not a wheel turns on this mill until McClure makes up every minute we've killed for him."

The Irishman looked into Ned's face. There had been the glimmer of an accusing look but it was gone. In its place was something big and honest that hushed the angry protest about to leap forth. Their eyes held for a moment, then the tankman's fell while the flush swept his face once again.

"I'll explain to the boys," said Ned, moving away toward the separator.

"No, lad," cried Easy, impulsively seizing his arm. "'Tis the hot curse I was nearly givin' ye. Ye're too white, Ned, fer a divil the loikes uv wan Easy Murphy. Shure 'tis right ye are, though I'm hatin' the idea. I'll hike till the mill and make me diplomatical defince before the gang. Sind me carcas till Belfast whin the boys git through wid ut."

Making a comical grimace, he set off to the separator to do the hardest thing he had ever attempted.

The men listened silently while Easy made his brief and self-accusative explanation. At the abrupt conclusion there resulted a most awkward pause. The gang were dumb at the unexpectedness of it. Each man was torn by several desires. He wanted to laugh, to howl, in fact. But something fine in him rendered him mute. There was a great admiration for their game boss and an even greater admiration for their game and artful culprit. The embarrassment had about reached the explosive point when Jean Benoit let out a scream.

"Ze res' do moche good, I tink," said he, shaking with laughter. "Wan, two, tree cheer on de boss an' dees ver bad Irish fellow."

At his words there broke out a jolly shout while the gang lay back on the straw and laughed to their heart's content.

Through the long wait there was not a murmur.

Meanwhile in McClure's gang consternation reigned. The last drop of water had been sucked up by the inspirator and the water was sinking in the glass. The men were perched on all vantage points on the lookout for the delinquent. No sign of him could they discover.

"Get Smithers to haul these barrels filled at the slough," directed McClure to Snoopy Bill, pointing to the barrels about the engine. "They'll keep her going until I can find that blankety Nick."

McClure had barely set off on his quest when one of the teamsters called the attention of the gang to the sudden "hang-up" of the Valley machine. As an hour passed and there was no sign of the Valley men resuming work, Snoopy Bill and his companions grew jubilant to a degree.

Nearly two hours later McClure appeared riding the tank and towing his buggy, in which lay the inebriate tanker.

A few minutes after, the Mogul was driving ahead under full pressure, joined shortly by the distant hum of the Valley Gang. Into the dark they raged, fighting ahead until eight, when the defiant whistles of the rival engines told that the great run was over.

VI

THE THRESHING CHAMPIONS

Louie Swale's restaurant was full, choked with threshers agog for the result of the great struggle. Almost every individual present had a stake involved. The building was a uniquely composite plant, comprising department store, café, bar, club, all under the solitary genius of the rotund and active Swale. He combined the offices of proprietor, manager, floor-walker, bartender, chef, cashier, possessing an innocent smile of friendliest amenity and the obsequious deportment of a suave head-waiter. He had certain periodic fines to meet for the vending of ancient beverages that fell without the code. These he paid promptly with sanguine light-heartedness. Louie Swale was universally liked, as are all good fellows whom careless Nature throws into life incomplete in the entire central osseous system of the vertebrate. He was a fat, juicy, even companionable earthworm.

The store carried a thorough line from roots to ribbons, occupying the front section of the building. Out of the store one wandered into a long room, low and rectangular, where Louie dispensed the quaffable and edible mysteries of his bar-café. The rear apartment was a blind room some twenty feet square, containing a few rough chairs and a round table covered with a green baize cloth. A well-thumbed pack on the centre of the table was the only purposeful article visible. There were two doors, both provided with heavy bars on the inside. One opened into the outshed; the other into the bar. This door was locally renowned as The Green Baize Door, and was believed to secrete behind its baize-covered panels a barrel of mysteries unco', cabalistic and otherwise. Since it was windowless, two dirty lamps did duty night and day. Obviously, when the "Square Room" was occupied seriously the Green Baize Door was to be found shut. At such times a peculiar knock was the sesame.

Store and café were crowded with men anxious to hear

the momentous decision of Jack Butte. Suddenly there arose a stamping and shouting. The stakeholder had climbed up on a table and was calling order. Glasses were set down and cards stacked.

"Gentlemen!" he cried. "There is a little preliminary or two I must pull off before I can announce the winner of the threshing bout between Rob McClure and Ned Pullar. Whatever the result, I appeal to the winners and losers to take their medicine. I want the word of both bosses that they will not stand for any sorehead business or rough house. I'll not hand out the totals until I get that word."

Butte paused significantly.

"Go ahead," said Ned, with a grin. "We'll be good."

"Agreed!" exclaimed McClure. "My gang is no bunch of squealers. Spit it out."

"Thank you, gentlemen," said Butte. "That is satisfactory. But there is another matter. Before I hand out the stakes I want you to choose two rank outsiders from this crowd who shall go into the Square Room with me and verify my figures. When they have made an audit I will come out and give you the facts."

Speedily the arrangement was effected and the three men went in behind the Green Baize Door.

During the interim Easy Murphy shuffled close to Snoopy Bill Baird. Grinning insolently into his face he addressed him in a cavernous stage whisper.

"How's the buttercups, Snoopy?" said he. "Ye did not consarn yersilf wid a second bokay."

Andy Bissett, standing near, placed his hand deterringly on Easy's shoulder.

"Steady, lad!" he whispered. "Ned's given his word. Keep in line."

Snoopy Bill ruffled instantly at the thrust. With a quick snatch at his breast pocket he drew out a bunch of bills and fluttered them flauntingly in Easy's face.

"How about a bokaa-y of these nice green shamrocks?" said he, with an exasperating laugh. "Have you the eye for a fresh fifty?"

"Indade, and they are the purty flowers," was the quick response. "They're to be had fer the pickin'. I'm wid ye, Snoopy."

Quickly he covered the bet, placing the stake with a bystander. The incident stimulated an emulation in the crowd, and by the time Butte appeared again the excitement had risen to the point of explosion.

"Hold your horses for a little!" he cried, smiling into the glaring eyes of the gamesters. "I'll go right to the point. For a month past these two gangs have been hammering away to roll up a big total, and I want to tell you they have done it. The gangs have worked twenty-seven full days and have made the record runs of the Pellawa country."

Butte's deliberate manner was too slow for his strained audience.

"Cut the talk, Jack! Cough up the totals!" yelled a voice.

"Hear, hear!" came an applauding roar.

"To resume," said Butte, bowing pleasantly, "in estimating the oats I reduced them to a total weight and then dividing by sixty, found the equivalent in weight of wheat. The total is therefore stated in terms of wheat. This was agreed upon by the two bosses. Rob McClure's machine has turned out a total of seventy thousand, eight hundred and twenty-one bushels."

At the announcement the McClure gang and their partisans lifted a shout of elation. Above the ensuing hubbub rose the brogue of Easy Murphy:

"Shure, Johnny Butte, 'tis a swell towtal. But ye'll hev till open yer mug wider, begobs, whin ye give the Valley count."

In spite of the extreme tension a boisterous roar greeted the defy.

"Against this," said the stakeholder amid a breathless silence, "the Valley Outfit have rolled up the huge total of seventy-one thousand, nine hundred and fifty-five bushels — —"

His words were drowned in a wild ringing cheer. Led by Murphy's deep bass roar, the Valley Outfit let go. As the rumpus died down Andy Bissett lifted his cap and shouted:

"Three cheers for Rob McClure's gang. They made a great run."

Ere they could raise the shout McClure yelled:

"No! Saw off your blankety howl. We want none of it. You doped one of my men or you would never have turned the trick."

Easy Murphy's lips were framing a reply when Ned spoke up.

"I want to state," said he with quiet deliberateness, "that as far as my knowledge goes, the Valley Gang has run this thing as straight as a whip. I appeal to Jack Butte. Do we win on our merits?"

A chorus of applause greeted Ned's words.

"Gentlemen!" replied the stakeholder. "This game has been run on the square. My figures have been verified and are open to the public. The Valley Outfit are the undisputed champions of The Qu'Appelle. Come up to the counter and I'll pay over the cash."

The convivial spirit ran high as the wagers were

collected. In the rear of the room McClure and his men held angry concourse. Suddenly they pushed their way to the counter. McClure spoke loudly, his face and eyes aflame.

"Come, Swale," commanded he. "We set up the drinks for the house. Make it hard stuff all round."

His manner was offensive. Ostensibly the host, he was really the bully. The Valley Outfit made no move to accept the proffered treat. Ned Pullar stepped up to his sullen opponent.

"No, Rob McClure!" was his crisp exclamation, accompanied by a flash of indignant eyes. "We don't drink with gentlemen who insult us in the same breath. The Valley Outfit, with their little thirty-six inch mill, beat you to a frazzle. You'll never have a chance like this again, for next fall will find The Qu'Appelle Champions capering about the finest mill on the Pellawa plains. You look, Rob, almost mad enough to fight. Very well. I have given Jack Butte my word to keep quiet. The Valley Outfit is going to get out and leave you the whole house. If you want to mix up with us, don't let us get away. If you are afraid of mussing up Louie's joint we'll wait for you outside. Meanwhile, will you accommodate us, gentlemen, by clearing away from that door?"

At the words he brushed past McClure, who stood glowering at him with eyes that streamed a liquid hate. For all his rage McClure was held from battle by a subtle enervation that baffled him.

"The Valley Outfit will leave at once," was Ned's cry as he flung open the door. With his hand on the knob he waited for his men to pass out before him. With surprising promptitude they complied. Easy Murphy was the last to leave. Pausing on the threshold he turned about.

"'Tis a braw bunch ye are, McClure, wid yer blower bunged and yer engine buckin'. Begobs, I cud put the howl gang uv ye till slape on a wathurr wagon. Come out intill the moonlight."

With that he went out, followed by a flying flask and the curses of McClure.

"Good-night, gentlemen!" said Ned, a mocking light in his eye. "We'll hang around outside for ten minutes or so. If you can make it, why—the Valley Outfit would be delighted."

Once out among his men they urged him to go back. But he shook his head.

"No, lads!" he said firmly. "I do not want to fight. If they come out we'll sail in. I think I've something better than even a good fight. I'll put you next when we pull away from Louie's."

The ten minutes passed. The door opened once but shut again. The Valley Gang hooted derisively. They waited five minutes longer. McClure had evidently passed up the challenge. Though his men knew it not, Ned was intensely relieved. He could scarcely understand. The fact was McClure apprised the situation exactly notwithstanding his rage. He was no coward; nor was he a fool. He knew that gang for gang Ned had him beaten in more ways than in the mere threshing. Let the Valley Outfit pull off its bluff. He would nurse his chagrin and strike—later.

When Ned got his men well out of ear-shot he addressed them in a sudden light-heartedness that surprised them.

"I want to thank you, lads, for holding yourselves so wonderfully when I know you were itching to get your hands on McClure and his oary-eyed crew. This is a great night. We've threshed Rob McClure twice to-night. We've out-milled him for a month and gathered in the wager and we've handed him a mighty hard punch by forcing him and his gang to funk. We are now going to pull off a little stunt that will be remembered for many a day along The Qu'Appelle. Easy will come with me. The rest of you get back to the caboose with Andy. He'll put you next. We'll meet you there at eleven o'clock. You will all remember that to-night's Hallowe'en."

By a mighty effort of self-restraint the men acceded to Ned's request to leave the village. Eleven o'clock found them waiting with Andy, all agog for the next move.

VII
HALLOWE'EN ON THE QU'APPELLE

At eleven o'clock McClure and his men staggered out of Swale's joint. For half an hour they prowled the streets, alarming the village with their wild whoops. At twelve they scrambled into their grain wagon and tore down the main street at a furious pace. Out to Smithers they raced, a roistering company of drunken fools.

Ned and Easy, posted among the poplars in the grove north of the barn, saw them ride into the barnyard. In the light of the moon the two men could see them tumbling out of the wagon, sprawling over each other, noisy and ill-humoured.

"I see Rob at the heads uv the horses," said Easy. "He niver goes home whin he's rale well pickled."

64

"We've got the whole crew at home, then," whispered Ned. "We are in luck. Come, let us round up the boys."

Slipping quietly away, they arrived at their own caboose.

Andy and the rest were awaiting them. Briefly Ned rehearsed his plans and was gratified to find them primed and ready to the last detail. In a few moments they set out for McClure's caboose. They carried planks, ropes, hammers and spikes, while Easy Murphy brought up the rear with his huge span of grays. The team was shrouded in great dark blankets with black nets covering their light heads. Each man was masked with his bandanna handkerchief, giving the marauders the appearance of a gang of bandits or a lynching posse.

At the edge of the grove they paused and listened intently. Not forty yards away stood the caboose with its crew of quarrelsome men. A confusing dialogue of altercations was in progress. After a time the men settled into their bunks, where the bibulous debate was drowsily maintained, finally simmering to the thick-tongued harangue of one persistent individual.

At a signal from Ned the Valley Outfit crept noiselessly upon their unsuspecting prey. Arrived at the caboose they made a swift survey. The farmstead was quiet. Smithers and his men were sound asleep. No interruption from that quarter. The caboose was the usual midget bunkhouse, a rectangular box on truck chassis with a bow roof. At the tongue end was a door. In the other end near the roof was a tiny window, too small for the exit of a man's body. Andy and his men stole around to the rear of the caboose. Striking one end of the plank solidly into the ground, they placed the other against the middle of the door. Two men held it in place while two swung their weight on it, holding the door shut as with a vise. McClure and his men were trapped. Quickly a stout plank was placed across the top of the door and nailed with five-inch spikes to the corner posts. Another plank was nailed similarly across the bottom, perfectly sealing the caboose.

By this time a commotion had arisen within. Snoopy Bill could be heard shaking the men and dragging them out of their bunks. Above the tumult soared McClure's heavy voice, disclosing in the angry vehemence of his curses a swift conclusion as to the identity of the assailants. Outside in the moonlight frolicked the masked figures. The excitement was intense. At Ned's desire all audible speech was to be suppressed. Easy Murphy was in his element and wanted to holler.

"Be the ghost uv me grandfahthurr!" he whispered to Jean Benoit. "'Tis the happiest hour since Oi left Owld Oireland."

Amid ill-suppressed laughter the freak proceeded. Backing his horses to the tongue, Easy speedily hitched on and pulled out of the barnyard. Long before Smithers and his men could wake and realize what had happened the big grays had spirited away the caged crew, surrounded by the triumphant body-guard of Valley threshers.

Urging his horses to a trot, Easy turned into the west road and bowled along merrily over ruts and stones to the fierce accompaniment of the pandemonium from within. Once a head unwisely protruded itself through the small opening only to receive a smart rap and to be instantly drawn in.

"Head across the Northwest Cut," directed Ned. "We'll run them up on Bald Hill, where they can get a good view

66

of the lake."

When the brow of the Cut was reached Easy reined in his horses.

"Shall we cross be the thrail," said he in a loud whisper to Ned, "or shall we bounce sthraight on over the rocky road till Dublin?"

"Give them the rocky road," was Ned's grim response.

"Begobs, yer a darlin'!" cried Easy, with a muffled whoopee as he swung the grays off the prairie down the side of the Cut.

Then began a half-mile of rocking and tossing, pitching over hillocks, boulders, badger holes and stumps, the caboose lurching about like a ship in a heavy sea and thoroughly churning up its human contents. The little bunkhouse became hideously vocal as execrations came forth, vengeful chorus from its tormented interior. Easy's eyes seemed to have uncanny vision for holes and hidden logs and jolting rocks, while the big grays, alarmed by the outrageous tumult, snorted wildly, plunging through everything with irresistible force.

The weird passage of the gulch was at length accomplished, winding up on the windy skull of Bald Hill.

"They'll have a very fine stretch of the valley to look into from here," said Andy with a grin, as his eyes took in the sweep of the hill.

"Indade, 'tis rale illigint," said Easy. "Rob wull be chargin' a nickel a pape from the bay window above."

"Unhitch the grays, Easy," said Ned, his eyes darting mischief. "We are not going to leave the caboose here. The fun is about to begin."

Ned's remark was cryptic. "If we are not going to leave them here, why unhitch?" was the query in every mind.

"Ah, Ned! 'Tis a darlin' I said ye wuz!" exclaimed Easy, seized by a sudden inspiration. He had tumbled to Ned's dark design. "Ye wull be afthur shootin' the shoot wid our frinds in the packin'-box?" was his sly guess.

"Hats off to our little boss!" cried Andy softly, shaking with laughter.

"By gar, dat cabooze yump on de lake lak beeg eggspress! Ha!" Jean forthwith "went up" venting his ecstasy in a series of handsprings.

When he came down he did what the rest were doing. He took a swift, keen glance at the hill. The slope fell rapidly away, dropping evenly hundreds of feet to the sandy shingle of the beach over a quarter of a mile away. Through a wide gap in the shore bluffs could be seen the silver shimmer of the waves. There could be but one end to the proposed flight of the caboose,—the cold, white bosom of the lake.

With deliberate thoroughness the Valley men made their preparations. The horses unhitched, the tongue of the caboose was roped high and locked firmly so that it could have no side swing. Then the men took their places about the wheels and rear.

"Just a minute!" whispered Ned. "One of you lads had better pull a watch on this thing. This old bus is in for her record run."

A chorus of subdued laughs rose above the noise emanating from the interior of the doomed vehicle.

"Shoulders to the wheels!" was Ned's low order. "Now, all together! Send her a-kiting."

Every man got down with a will and a smothered yo-heave started the caboose down the slope. With a final united shove they sent it away from their hands in mad career toward the lake. Down the hill it sped, swaying in its course like a drunken man, but heading straight for the water. In fearfully accelerated speed it shot over the short sand beach and crashed in the gleaming waves. Carried along by its great momentum it charged the lake like a racing motor-boat, throwing a huge prow wave as it ran into the deep water. Weighted with its heavy truck and human freight it sank almost half-way to the roof before coming to a standstill.

While the caboose sped down the hill the perpetrators of the deed watched its flight in breathless interest. As it plunged into the water a cheer roared down the hillside.

Meanwhile in desperate rage and no small alarm McClure with his gigantic strength had torn a hole in the roof and thrusting his shoulders upward broke through and climbed out just as the car came to rest in the bed of the lake. Looking up the moonlit hill he could plainly see the group of men crowning its height and caught the cheer that swept down. No word, however, escaped him. Thoroughly sobered, the full significance of the daring lark burst upon him, sealing his lips. There were times when Rob McClure was unexpectedly silent. Reaching down he helped his men one by one out to safety. Soon the roof was black with men.

"Dey some leetle drown rat!" exclaimed Jean Benoit, shaking with laughter at the sight. "What dey goin' to do?"

Through the quiet air came the answer. It was McClure's voice.

"I guess there is nothing else for it," said he.

Instantly came the sound of a splash. Other splashes followed and then could be seen a straggling line of dark figures plunging through the surf.

"Now let them have it," cried Ned.

With all the vigour of seventeen pairs of powerful lungs

they lifted cheer after cheer.

"Enough!" cried Ned at last. "This beats a fight. We have licked the whole gang without anybody getting mussed up. The cold water will help to sober them."

A moment later Bald Hill was bare.

VIII
THE RIVAL BOSSES

McClure sat in his office nursing his choler, with a face bitterly inexorable. The routine of threshing moved on. Looking through the window, as upon a former occasion, he saw the two lines of smoke trailing off together over the fields. The sight caused a tightening of jaws. For an hour he had sat moodily thus, plunged in gloom.

The loss of the heavy wager was not desirable and the defeat galled. But it was not this that caused the baleful smouldering within the eyes. He tossed away the stake with the sang-froid of the gamester. He would get it back when the luck turned. The thing that incensed him was not the utter rout but the manner of it. His shoulders had been pinned to the mat by the swift address of an antagonist he had despised. The conviction sank in upon him that this young and resourceful foe had toyed with him. This levity was the barb that inflamed the wound.

The episode of Hallowe'en was a cup of gall to him. The kidnapping and ducking of himself and gang was a daring act deep and wily in its deliberate insolence. He fancied he caught the mocking laugh on Pullar's face. Ned had used him for a public burlesque. The caboose still lay in the lake. Pellawa was highly amused and—talking. Defeat was complete and bitter. Added to this was the condemnatory voice of an inner and subtle monitor that told him he had been wrong from the start and moreover had not scrupled to foul his man. His opponent on the other hand had played fair. These facts did not trouble the conscience of Rob McClure. They nettled him. He resented the alignment of public opinion with his adversary. He would use the same tactics again. But he would see to it that the camouflage was perfect. The longer he brooded the deeper grew his dour morosity. Vengeance cried loudly within him. He vowed a tenfold reprisal. Some day he would put on a burlesque himself and then — —

Suddenly he was roused from his malignant reveries by a light step outside the door. In a moment it opened quietly, admitting Helen McClure. Her face so compellingly attractive had a tragic weariness in it. A close observer wondered at the acute pain that would glance at times from the clear eyes. Neither the beauty of her fragile person nor the remarkable dignity of her bearing could hide the reality of suffering. Rob McClure, man of steel though he was, secretly acknowledged the noble strength of his wife. In a soft voice she announced:

"Mr. Pullar wishes to see you, Rob." Turning to the newcomer she smiled brightly, inviting him in. Motioning him to a chair she withdrew.

Ned remained standing.

"Sit down," said McClure coldly.

"No, thank you!" returned Ned courteously. "My business will be brief. Man to man I want to know whether or not you are satisfied with Jack Butte's decision."

71

McClure darted a swift look into the other's eyes.

"It is a mere trifle," said he with a deprecatory gesture. "Butte is straight. You got the lucky breaks."

"Very good!" said Ned. "It gratifies me to hear you say it. You positively agree that the Valley Outfit win?"

"You got the lucky breaks," repeated McClure.

"That satisfies me," said Ned conclusively as he took a package from his breast pocket. Reaching forward he placed the bundle on the desk before McClure. His eyes flashed and his voice had a ring of steel as he said:

"That is your share of the wager just as it was handed to me by Butte. You will remember, I think, that I did not desire to take up your bet. There is your cash. I will not touch the winnings. Gaming is the expedient of a lazy thief willing to take a chance. You can keep the swag. It is yours. Or—you can burn it. This completes my business. I wish you good-day."

McClure was astounded. His eyes dropped amazedly to the package before him. For a full minute he stared at the wad of ragged edged bills. Then into his face flooded a black tide. His hands clenched, clutching in a horrible convulsion of rage.

"You insolent devil!" he cried fiercely, hurling the package to the floor. Turning he flashed angry eyes about, surprised to find that he was alone in the room. He leaped to his feet, nonplussed, baffled. His eye caught a motion outside the window. It was Ned unhitching his horse from the post not thirty yards away. At sight of his enemy a fearful idea came to him. Reaching down swiftly he opened a drawer and snatching out a revolver broke open its blue chambers. There was a gleam of brass rims. It was loaded. With a menacing cry he stepped to the window and threw up the sash. He was dropping the sight on the tall figure when his ear caught the tripping of light feet along the hall. It was Mary coming to his room. He held the gun on his target for the briefest instant, then dropped the muzzle and thrust it covertly into his pocket. As he whirled about Mary burst through the door, a lithe, little figure in riding boots, sombrero and habit. She looked at him, her face radiant, her eyes dancing with the joy of living. He seemed hesitant. Could it be that for once her father was inviting? With a happy cry she closed upon him. He smiled a strange, relieved smile.

"Daddy! Daddy!" she cried delightedly. "I have had such a glorious ride. Bobs pranced down the trail a thing of wildest life, making the trip from The Craggs in less than an hour."

Throwing her arms about his neck she drew his head gently to her. Swept off his feet by the swift dénouement of the last few minutes, he submitted to her will. For the first time in years she felt the absence of chilling repulse. Holding him close in her ecstasy she kissed his forehead again and again. With a final caress she laid her cheek against his for one silent, happy moment, then broke away and ran off to her room thrilling with pleasant emotion.

Mary McClure did not know that her glad arrival had held her father's hand from an unspeakable crime. He was indeed grateful to her for the interposition, though his face showed no repentance. There was, though, a regretful pang in the breast. It was caused not by any faint penitence for his evil design but by the memory of Mary's cheek against his. The "feel" of her soft, tender touch was there. For some strange reason the memory of it sank deep. The sound of her footsteps had scarcely died away, however, when the old ruthlessness returned. The relief he now felt was that of one who had been saved from committing a violent inexpediency. Glancing through the window he saw the horseman cantering leisurely down the trail. As he watched the hard lines drew about his mouth. He began casting about for the package of money, finding it at length near the door. Picking it up he looked at it a moment with bright eyes that acknowledged an enigma. Walking to the window he looked out, smiling secretively and shaking the wad ominously at the Valley boss.

"It will help to break you, Pullar," was his threat.

Going to the desk he opened a large drawer and deposited the money carefully in a tin box.

Above in her room Mary watched Ned ride out of sight into the Valley. She was greatly mystified as to the purpose of his visit. She regretted missing a meeting with him, but reflected with deepest happiness on the friendliness of her father. The moment, she felt, was full of happy augury.

IX

A LAND SHARK

Reddy Sykes had drifted into Pellawa during the early weeks of summer. Though at first an anomaly in the little town, the citizens grew used to his presence. It was hard to define Sykes' business. He was not a lawyer, though he had a distinctly legal turn of mind. He had acquired the title of Commissioner. He began work in the village with a command of considerable capital. His most lucrative line was real estate. He bought and sold farms and manipulated the transfer of large acreage blocks. A few city shingles decorated his window but the great urban boom of the West was as yet on the verge and the subdivisional mania had not got properly under way. The ability of the new arrival in his selected field was so surprising and apparent that his presence in Pellawa was a poser to the shrewd minds of the plains. He could have made things hum in a bigger world.

Personally, Sykes was a character that invited scrutiny. He was comparatively young, still in the early thirties, possessing a full-blooded interest in life. His face was unusually hard for so young a man and wore an habitual calculating expression. He was a man of scheme and intrigue. His motion as he moved about was very like that of Reynard as he slunk through the night en route to Mr. Farmer's chicken coop. He lived by his wits, searching the trail closely for tracks of his prey. His nose was always in the wind. He was alert for the lucky cast of the die that should tumble fortune into his lap. Inventive and resourceful, his mind stored a great fund of premises. He could adopt and discard twenty viewpoints in as many minutes. The stolid, common-place farmers fought shy of Sykes, shunning his speciousness, afraid of a snare. They felt the unrelenting, unscrupulous thing in the man, though unable to detect it in his handsome face.

Notwithstanding the diffidence of the farmers to enter into free commerce with the real estate agent he had become an accepted cog in the social wheel. He had made one powerful friend—Rob McClure. The two drew together like steel and magnet. The attraction fused into an implicit partnership from the very start. There was a reason for this, a matter on which Rob McClure was utterly in the dark.

Only one person in the settlement had even surmised it. Reddy Sykes was dominated by the mightiest of human motives in his facile address at fostering a strong friendship with McClure. Ned Pullar alone understood that he was at once lured by the passion of love and urged by the fell ardour of hate. The object of his regard was Mary McClure. The object of his rancour, Ned himself. He had effected his purpose with McClure by an ingratiating cunning assisted by an unusual mutual attraction. His relations with Mary and Ned ran back into the cross currents of their university life. Of that again.

Sykes' friendship with McClure opened to him the McClure home. He availed himself of the hospitality in a wise and restrained use of the privilege. His reception had been cordial. The two women were only too glad to promote goodwill with a friend of Rob's. Helen McClure was always pleased to welcome the gentlemanly guest. Mary in her secret mind was very considerably perturbed, remembering certain advances made by Sykes in the past. She had turned him down on occasion and once had deservedly and effectually snubbed him. She was agreeably surprised, however, at his casual gallantries. He was courteous and companionable, but did not in the faintest degree press his attentions.

Sykes had been moving about his office studying closely certain realty maps of local townships. His search over, he sat down at his desk and picking up a letter read it carefully. This was the third perusal. He was pondering some undoubtedly alluring proposition. In his mouth he held an unlit cigar, rolling it around in unconscious habit, occasionally chewing off the end and throwing it away. Looking through the window out upon the street he saw something that brought sudden resolution into his eyes. Andy Bissett was dashing by with his team of blacks. He pulled up in front of a store and hurriedly tied his horses to a post. He was about to enter the store when Sykes hailed him. Andy walked over and entered the office.

"How's the Valley Outfit?" inquired Sykes pleasantly.

"Laid up with a broken shaft," was the reply.

"I've been looking out for you to-day, Bissett," said Sykes affably, plunging into business. "I want you to read this."

He handed over the letter he had just been reading.

"This," said he, "is a communication from a farmer in Northern Alberta who is anxious to get hold of a farm in this settlement. He owns a section and is willing to swap it for an improved half in the Pellawa district. The full description of the land is there. It is a big snap."

Andy read the letter rapidly then handed it back.

"I have nothing I would care to exchange for that," said he quietly.

"How about the quarters you are renting to the Poles?"

Andy shook his head.

"Not in the market."

"Some of your friends might consider the proposition."

"No," said Andy decidedly, "I could not recommend the deal to any of my friends. Personally I do not like it."

Sykes looked up sharply with the Reynard-like movement.

"This is an A-1 chance, a windfall for somebody."

"It may be," agreed Andy dubiously. "It seems to me unusual. Aside from that, however, it is not the snap it appears."

Sykes' voice sounded a shade metallic as he said:

"How do you make it?"

Andy noted the change in tone but continued pleasantly:

"In the first place this land about Pellawa is simply wonderful. That other may be good. Then again there is a pretty fast movement up in this Valley land. We are expecting it to skyrocket. Things are promising hereabouts. I think it will be well to stick."

"Still," objected Sykes, "the difference in acreage is great. It covers all rise."

"That may be. Who can tell? That point would have to be settled by a personal visit to the Alberta farm."

Sykes shifted his cigar impatiently, biting it viciously.

"How about Pullar?" he queried carelessly. "He might swap the homestead. He is young yet—just the age to pitch into a section of virgin land. Pullar's the man."

"You mean Ned?" said Andy.

"Of course."

"Ned would not consider the matter for a minute."

"Why?"

"That land is his father's. Ned is manager and real head, but the land is still deeded to his father. Although the old man has desired to make all or any part over to the boy, Ned would not agree."

Sykes seemed to muse on the matter a moment. Andy did not notice the cunning light flash into the other's eyes. His companion's quick mind had gathered something of great interest to him.

"The fact is," said Andy deliberately, "I would not recommend this to any friend of mine, as I have said."

Suddenly a resentful light burned in Sykes' eyes.

"Do you mean to say you will knock this deal?" said he.

"Sure," said Andy smiling. "I'll knock it into a cocked hat if anybody appeals to me."

"Say!" said Sykes, the lash of sarcasm entering into his tone. "You rubes carry some side, eh? A few of you little farmers think you can chin-up to Reddy Sykes. Bah!"

He turned on his heel.

With a cheerful "Good-day!" Andy took his departure.

Looking at the figure crossing the street Sykes smiled sardonically.

"Much obliged, Bissett!" was his muttered soliloquy. "You were easy. Ha! It looks pretty good! Pretty good to me!"

Late that night McClure appeared in the office.

"Anybody with you?" inquired Sykes, looking up as he entered.

"No. I am alone," was the response. "Took a skip in to get a line on business. Anything new?"

For answer Sykes thrust the letter into his hand. McClure recognized the source instantly.

"He has located another spot, I see."

Sykes nodded.

Looking up from the letter McClure ruminated for a moment.

"There's good money in these transfers if we can get them going. That's where good fishing comes in."

"Tried Bissett to-day," observed Sykes ruefully.

"It was no go?"

"No."

"Keep away from Bissett," was McClure's low counsel. "There are easier prospects. If not we'll have to chuck it."

"Chuck nothing!" was Sykes' incisive ejaculation. "This community's full of suckers. There are droves of easy rubes hereabouts fairly howling, 'Come touch me up.'"

For a moment McClure rubbed his chin reflectively. Sykes eyed him closely.

"I know what you are hunting down," said he, looking McClure full in the eye. "You're on just one trail these days. You are tracking the boss of the Valley Outfit."

McClure looked up surprised.

"I see I've hit it," resumed Sykes with a laugh. "Bissett put me next a little fact that has a whole barrelful of possibilities. He informs me that Pullar's three-quarter sections are all in the old man's name."

McClure shook his head.

"Don't believe it. Ned's too good a head to stand for that."

"It's a fact, just the same," maintained Sykes. "Bissett told me all about it."

"What if it is?"

"I guess you know old Ed. Pullar. Thirsty old guy at times."

McClure laughed wisely.

"That's the point," said Sykes in a whisper. "We have an even chance of getting him there."

McClure said nothing, but Sykes, watching him from the foxy crevices of his half-shut eyes, knew that he had probed a mighty impulse in his companion. The gloating of anticipated revenge looked out of Rob McClure's great eyes. He was roused from his baleful reverie by the voice of Sykes.

"That prospect pleases you, Rob," said he in a significant tone that drew the swift glance of McClure. "And I am with you to the limit provided——"

He paused and looked peculiarly at the other. McClure was puzzled.

"Provided," resumed Sykes, "you do the same with me."

"You have me guessing, Reddy."

"You do not know what I am driving at?"

McClure shook his head.

"Then I'll set you right. For some years I have known the daughter of Rob McClure. All these years I have regarded her as the one thing desirable. That is why I am out among the rubes. She has never been more gracious than since my arrival here. You stand by me there and I'm with you. You can do a lot."

The two men looked long into each other's eyes. Then McClure's gaze became abstract and far away. He was seeing something other than Sykes' glittering eyes. He saw Mary as she burst in upon him the day of his interview with Ned. He felt the soft touch of her cheek. Suddenly he was recalled to the issue.

"Well?" was the crisp challenge.

"Go right in and win," said he with a strange smile. "Do it right and I'm agreeable. So far as I know you have a clear field. You can count on me."

"You think the field is open?" said Sykes.

"There isn't a doubt. I know all about my girl."

Sykes smiled and let it go at that. There was some information he could impart to this cocksure father but it would be more serviceable later. He reflected for a moment on the effect of the disclosure that Ned Pullar was very much in the field. Then he smiled again, conscious of holding a rather high hand.

McClure could see no untoward possibility and was satisfied.

So they made the compact.

X

THE DREAMER

The watcher stepped back into the shelter of the maples. She had emerged from them but a moment before and had been on the point of addressing the worker when her capricious will deterred her. She was looking upon the great figure of a man. He was aged, nearing the fullness of the allotted span. His shoulders, however, were square and his back straight. His form rose to a towering height, retaining its lines of strength and was crowned by a shapely head with its resplendent glory of long white hair. The face was noble with a touch of gentleness. The intelligent eyes had a masterful light mingling with the dreaminess of them, while his cheeks had the soft rotundity of a child's and the roses of a girl. Before her stood the father of Ned Pullar. Often had she heard of him. This was the first time she had really beheld him. She was very surprised, agreeably so.

The old man was busy flailing a bag of chaff. So absorbed was he in his employment that he was rudely startled when a woman's voice accosted him gently.

"Mr. Pullar, I believe!"

Looking up suddenly he detected a small girlish figure in white. Her face was attractive with a bright friendliness that set him instantly at ease.

"I am highly honoured," was his reply as he set down his stick and bowed with courtly stateliness. "Is it the little teacher I have the pleasure of greeting?"

"I am Mary McClure!"

The old man walked over and held out his hand with Western hospitality.

"Welcome to The Craggs, lassie. The lad, Ned, has been telling me much about you. Will you not sit down?"

He placed a rustic chair before her.

"I have been waiting for you to call on your new neighbour," said Mary with a smile as she accepted the proffered chair. "But you have not favoured us yet. I am afraid you will find me a very impatient and exacting neighbour, Mr. Pullar."

His eyes twinkled at her speech.

"Well now, that is a pretty rub," said he amusedly. "I shall have to hunt up my visiting cards and call around."

"Now, see that you do," was the girl's reply as she shook an accusing finger at him. "But you must not entertain now, Mr. Pullar. I came over to watch you at work. I am curious to know why you were belabouring that poor sack so roundly."

The old man laughed delightedly.

"I will tell you all about it," was the reply. "I am threshing the wheat that is in it."

"But why do you have to do that with a stick? Is Ned not the best thresher along the Valley?"

A proud look came into the old man's eyes.

"Do you think so, lass?"

"Indeed I do. And so does the whole settlement."

"It is so, I believe," was the frank agreement. "But Ned does not thresh this. Those bags are filled with rare wheat heads selected from our head-row plots. For them I use the flail."

He had pointed to where a line of a dozen bulging

84

grain sacks swung on a stout rope between posts.

Mary's eyes opened.

"Mr. Pullar," said she engagingly, "I have heard most interesting rumours of what a wizard you are with seeds. One man told me solemnly that he believed you could grow a good crop in a field of dry dust. Is it true that you have developed a new variety of wheat?"

For a moment the old man did not answer. Instead he read earnestly the beautiful, vivacious face of the girl and the eyes deep in their intelligence.

"I believe, lassie, you would understand," was his satisfied reflection. "Would you like to hear the truth about The Red Knight?"

Mary looked steadily into the eyes above her. She did not comprehend the meaning of his question but she was fascinated by the noble enthusiasm that swept over the fine old face.

"Tell me. Will you?" was her soft voiced reply.

"Come with me," said he. "I will show you something."

The tone of his voice deeply impressed her. She knew that she was about to venture into the sacred recesses of a life. She followed him to the porch where rested a tub. Seizing the handle he pulled it out into the sunlight. Lifting a covering he disclosed to her eyes a mass of grain — beautiful wheat, brown-gold in colour, with the wealthy red tinge that tints the peerless milling kernel. The plump, red berries suggested to her heaps of tiny, golden pebbles. She was astonished and silent.

"It is The Red Knight," said he simply, stooping and dipping up a handful. She observed how fondly he held it in the palm of his great hand.

"It is very dear to you," was her gentle remark.

Once again he studied her eyes. They looked up at him with a clear-eyed rapture that provoked his grateful confidence.

"Come, lassie! Rest while I tell you the tale of the finding of The Red Knight.

"It will be forty years, come Maytime again, since I brought Kitty Belaire from the old East over the Valley of The Qu'Appelle to The Craggs. Here we set up a home in the little log hut you can see at the end of the lane. In the log hut was born the first wee bairn. He did not stay with us long and we laid him away in the dip beyond the bluffs. There, too, Ned came to us, filling the sore spot in our hearts left by his little brother. We were happy, the three of us, though we had little to do with, and the work was hard. The years were years of struggle. We fought the winds and the drought, rust, smut, hail and the frost with little success to boast about. One year we had a bumper crop with prices low. Then followed one or two without a harvest. Ned was growing to be a husky little chap when a crop grew on the place that promised us a forty-bushel yield. But one day a black cloud swept over the homestead and in ten minutes it was gone. We had no seed. On the heels of the hail came a drought year. Following it appeared a crop that filled the settlement with hope. We were getting ready to cut when a blight appeared. The rust reduced the yield from forty bushels to five. So passed the years and the battle went against us, with the frost the worst enemy of all. One terrible harvest it came to me that the seed was wrong. It matured too slowly. What we needed was a seed that would come along fast enough to harden before the blight of the rust or the nip of frost. The following harvest I set out on a quest. One day I discovered a patch of ripe heads among the filling grain. Upon shelling them I found a plump kernel fully matured. I plucked the strange heads and carefully preserved the wheat. When seeding time came round again I sowed them on a bit of new ground in the garden. They came up strong and far outstripped the other grain. I had great hopes. Filling time arrived and I watched developments. It was now plain to me that the new variety would ripen fully two weeks ahead of the old type. Then, in the depths of night, a crashing hailstorm and—my precious plot smashed into the earth.

"I had made the fatal mistake of not preserving a few kernels against accident. But that was the beginning. Henceforth I was alert to discover any quickly maturing plants among my fields of grain. By hand selection I began to improve the standard varieties. By use of head-row plots I was able to provide myself with a purer seed. But it took a great deal of time. My neighbours began to surpass me in quantity of yield. Eventually they regarded me as luny. At last only Kitty and Ned believed in me. They never failed me. They became experts in seed selection. They helped me with their sympathy. Together we made thousands of tests. Gradually we caught our feet. One year we started cutting a full week ahead of the settlement. We had escaped the rust and showed a plump sample. We were alone in our good fortune. From that time we were the first into the binding, our yield was at the top, and under Ned's wise management our quantity began to pull ahead, always showing a consistently high sample.

"It is four years this harvest that Kitty and the lad went out on a 'roguing' stalk. Perhaps you do not know that a 'rogue' is a foreign variety of grain that has appeared for some reason in your field. The task of plucking these 'rogues' is called 'roguing.' Upon their return the mother handed to me a headed plant of wheat carefully lifted from the ground. How well I remember it! She gave it into my hands with a smile.

"'Here, Edward!' she said brightly. 'Here is your Red Knight at last. I found him growing in the twenty acre field on the little knoll.'

"I took the plant and carefully examined it. The straw was strong and erect, the roots the most perfect I had ever looked upon. But it was the head that caught my eye, as it had caught Kitty's and Ned's. It was not exceptionally large but well compacted and heavy, its spikelets packed with wonderful kernels. We were not led into fond hopes by the remarkable heads, as we had tested many another apparently as perfect."

Here the old man paused, lost a moment in reverie.

"That winter the Mother died," resumed he softly. "But she left a legacy that will forever bless mankind. We carried out our tests. We have put The Red Knight through every conceivable trial and it remains pure, repeating its superior qualities each harvest. It is of the highest milling grade, grows a strong straw and erect, compact head, maturing three full weeks before any other wheat. This tub is filled from our head-row plots with the very purest Red Knight. In addition Ned has already cut and threshed a five acre field. The yield has been true to promise and will astonish the world. Red Knight, the gift to the world of Kitty Belaire, has averaged this year over one hundred bushels to the acre."

As the old man finished a deep silence fell on them, broken at length by Mary. At the first accents of her voice her companion looked up. He was surprised to see tears in her eyes.

"Mr. Pullar!" she said hesitantly, her voice touched with awe. "You and Ned and—his mother are—gracious benefactors. You are bringing a wonderful boon to the West —to the whole world."

Leaning forward the old man looked eagerly into the earnest eyes before him.

"Ah, lassie," he said kindly, "you are a wonderful little soul. You are seeing deep into this thing, God bless you. 'Tis a vision the three of us have had. The Red Knight will mean a steady and reliable living for the farmers round about us and a sure crop for the struggling pioneer in the new places of the world. It will mean that a million homesteads will spring up in the great Northern plains where men could scarcely live because of the rust and frost. It will fill up the bread-basket of the world and make cheaper food for the hard-pressed masses, for The Red Knight will push the grain belt three hundred miles nearer to the poles the whole world round."

"Just a moment, Mr. Pullar!" exclaimed Mary, seized by a brilliant idea. "I've got it! I believe every word you say. It is true. Gloriously true! But the world will have to hear about it. It will take time to marshall the forces of The Red Knight and start him on his great crusade. You will have to declare him to the world. The discovery and mission of this wonderful new wheat must be placed before the public, and at once."

"Ah," said he, "you speak the truth. Ned and I have thought it over, but we have no gift of the pen whatever."

Another deep silence fell over them. It was Mary who broke it once more.

"Do you think, Mr. Pullar," she said diffidently, "that—

that I could help you? I have done a little writing. We could get the facts into shape and some editor could put them in form for presentation to the public."

The old man looked at her with eyes in which glowed a grateful wonder.

"You believe my story enough to do that, lassie?"

"Why, of course! It is simply wonderful! Come over to the school each day at noon and we can work at the tale of The Red Knight while the children are playing. An hour a day will accomplish a great deal in a month. Will you come?"

Her companion reflected deeply before replying.

"It is a noble offer," he said gratefully. "But I will think it over. If I decide it is best I will come to-morrow."

"Thank you, Mr. Pullar!" was the pleased reply. "This has been an amazing hour. But I must be going. You will be sure and come?"

Waving good-bye she vanished through the trees.

For a long time the man reflected on the happy interview. At length he returned to the sack of unthreshed wheat. Picking up the flail he held it poised ready while his gaze grew pathetically reminiscent.

"Ah, Kitty," he whispered. "'Tis an angel she is. Our dreams will come true after all, dear heart."

XI

THE THIRD RIDER

Margaret Grant paced the terrace, her black hair flowing in

the wind. The sun flooded the Valley with a prodigal outpouring of his golden tanks. The girl's eyes snapped with the vivacity of life, for the world was streaming with light and the birds were carolling in joyous abandon. Something in the bubbling wildness of the morning lent a nimbleness to her feet, and she would change her sedate walk for a tripping scurry across the lawn. She cast frequent glances over the gorge to the Peak of the Buffalo Trails in evident anticipation of some appearance there. While she waited she let her eyes sweep down the Valley, her heart and ofttimes her feet dancing with the sun.

Margaret was a child of The Qu'Appelle. The gleaming valley had nursed her through childhood, writing the beauty of hill and stream and wind and sun into the little girl, making her skin as brown as that of the metis maiden, her blood warm and red and her soul free with the purity of the flashing light. She loved the cottonwoods and the poplars and the clustering, glistening birch, while the oak and willow folk cast a spell over her. She knew the berry and cherry trees and the sun-steeped slopes where browned the sweetest hazelnuts. Ask her where coquettes the wine-black saskatoon or the wonder berry—and she can tell. As for the flowers, the bees and Margaret were twin possessors. Equally dear were the people of feather and fur.

The lake was a fascinating, joyous mystery, whether it lay under her eyes a thing of shimmering light or frowning shadows. Its magic swept her most powerfully. In the moments of its hush, when it became a great calm silence, rippleless and infinitely deep, a new vastness with its own blue sky and clouds and shapely hills.

Far out in the lake lay a tiny island tufted with cottonwood shrubs and one ragged scrub oak. This tree had grown out of a crevice in the rock. The island was nothing more than a huge boulder and the bower of cottonwoods and bit of turf held precariously to the smoothed surface. Here the girl enjoyed the dulcet music of the waves and the solitude, reaching the island easily by aid of her birch canoe. From its behaviour in time of tempest this lonely spot had received the name of The Storm Rock. Long before the waves had worked into rollers an angry cloud of white spray above the rock portended the fury of the storm.

Suddenly the girl paused in her walk and fastened her eyes on the Peak of the Buffalo Trails. A glimmer of white crowned the Peak. She gave an exclamation of delight as she defined the form of Bobs. Astride was Mary McClure. A signal passed between the girls. Turning slightly, Margaret swept the north bank with a keen glance, emitting another ejaculation as she saw a rider cantering along the shoulder of the hill making his way down into the valley.

"Ned!" she observed, with a droll tip of her head. "You are remarkably punctual, my fine fellow. You need not push Darkey so fast, however, for Flash and I are going to take a very considerable time to saddle up."

Turning about, she glanced up at the Peak again. Bobs and his rider had disappeared. As she continued to look at the empty summit she was surprised to see another rider trot out on the hill. It was a man, and he halted his horse in the identical place where Mary had sat Bobs but a moment before. He looked over the valley toward the Grant homestead, then turning, vanished hurriedly down the hill.

The watcher was at a loss to account for the appearance of the strange rider. She pondered a moment.

"One of Blythes' cow-punchers!" was her conclusion. "He is probably beating up strays."

Satisfied and relieved at her surmise she ran into the house to prepare for the ride to Willow Glade.

Ned rode swiftly along, skirting the lake about the Pellawa end. He had an hour of fast riding before he at length disappeared into the groves near the brook. As he broke into the Glade he saw Bobs tied to a tree and his mistress seated on the log beside the stream.

"Ho, ho! Darkey!" he cried softly. "High fortune is ours!"

Bobs tossed his head in equine friendliness, but the figure on the log was absorbed in a study of the tree-tops. Tying his horse, Ned stole up on the silent one.

"Room for another on the observation car?" called Ned in her ear.

With a casual "Good-day, Ned!" she glanced into his eyes. Her face was so irresistibly teasing that he seized her hands.

"I am welcome, Mary?" said he.

Her reply was smothered by his lips. When conditions had become normal once more she announced importantly:

"I came here to-day, Ned, with the deliberate purpose of having an interview with you."

"That is delightfully gratifying," was the reply. "But since I know the lady so well I fear there is another reason forthcoming."

"We are to have a chaperon," resumed Mary. "I signalled Margaret from the Peak of the Buffalo Trails. She will be here—within—an hour or two. Flash has taken to loitering, I fear."

"Yes, we know what a sleepy nag Flash can be when Margaret has so made up her mind."

"You speak as though there is a little plot on foot."

"Rather on four feet, Mary."

Catching his eye Mary laughed.

"But there is another reason?" was his serious question. "Are you in trouble, Mary?"

"No," was her reply. "I am deeply interested in some one other than Mr. Pullar, Jr. And also in a number of things— the Red Knight, for example. Why have you not come over to the school sometimes with your father?"

He looked into her eyes with a frankness that satisfied her. She nodded comprehendingly.

"You did right," said she gently. "We agree that it was best. But I have wanted to consult you about the Red Knight. I think it is such a big, wonderful thing, and it means so much to your father. Do you— —"

Further speech was suddenly interrupted by a commotion in the woods. Bobs gave a vigorous whinny to which Darkey responded in a half-frightened way while both horses moved restively about their trees, nostrils distended and ears pricked forward.

"What can be troubling the horses?" said Mary looking about.

A careful scrutiny of the trees and underbrush failed to discover anything unusual.

"Probably a fox or a wolf," surmised Ned. "The brute was bold to come so near. The horses have become aware of some marauder."

They let it go at that, little thinking that the horses had a surprising reason for their unrest. For five minutes past a shadow had been slipping through the dense growth running toward the lake and had chanced a flit of a half dozen yards in the open to a clump of willows within a rod of the log on which they sat. Screened in the low trees lurked the crouching figure of Reddy Sykes. It was a fox,

94

indeed, a human fox that had agitated Bobs and his companion. The face of the agent was uncouth in its strange determination and jealousy. Waiting until quiet was restored he parted the leaves and took a glance at the objects of his bold espionage. At sight of the lovers his face went white and a wave of passion swept over him. As Mary resumed the conversation he listened with an eagerness wild and intense.

"I was saying," said Mary, "that The Red Knight has a powerful interest for your father."

"I am sure you discovered that easily," returned Ned.

"Yes. It is as dear to him as life itself. No mother could lavish more fondness upon her babe than your father does upon this marvellous new wheat."

"And because it means so much to Dad," said Ned gently, "it means even more to me. Yet I, too, am foolish over The Red Knight. I wonder can any one understand how it is that the roots of this plant go back so deep into the lives of Dad and me? It has grown out of the hard, glorious years. It is the one living thing linking our dear dead to us. Mary! It is my little mother's forget-me-not. The tenderest sentiment gathers about The Red Knight."

Mary laid her hand gently on his arm.

"Ned," she said, looking at him with the shine of dew in her eyes, "you will always foster this dear foolishness, will you not?"

Drawing her to him he kissed lips and cheeks and hair.

"I know you will," was her glad cry.

"But there is the other side," said Ned in a little. "The Red Knight is as astonishing a discovery for the good of the world as was steam in its application to transportation and industry. This is how Dad views it. Like the discovery of a new element it should be retained for the common human good. If controlled by the commercial interests and monopolists it will be lost. The Red Knight needs the care of the keenest and surest cultural science as well as the protection of a wise government. This new variety of wheat is very precious now or will be when the great experts have repeated the tests put through by Dad and myself. By spring, should our own experiments satisfy the competent judges, every bushel of Red Knight would be worth one hundred dollars. Forty thousand dollars! It sounds fabulous to farmers who have spent a lifetime in the fight to catch their feet. Dad, however, will not sell it in that way. He intends to distribute his unique seed in such a way as to insure its preservation and reproduction. Each bushel will go to a source that meets with his entire approval. Some will pay the hundred dollars per bushel, not that a monopolist's price may be realized but that the recipient may be impressed with the rare pricelessness of The Red Knight. Others will pay but a pittance. The great national farms will not be overlooked. It is Dad's purpose that when harvest rolls round again there will be from thirty to forty thousand bushels of Red Knight in the hands of the National Government and a corps of splendid farmers. They will agree to keep Red Knight pure and further improve his singular qualities by faithful selection and experiment."

As Ned finished speaking a deep silence fell on them, broken at length by Mary.

"That four hundred bushels of Red Knight is precious in many ways, Ned," said she. "You have taken precaution to protect it from harm?"

"We are doing our best to avoid misfortune. We have broken the bin up into three. There are two hundred bushels in the house; we have one hundred in the big granary and the balance is isolated in one of our galvanized-iron, portable bins set in the centre of a large ploughed field. This should provide for the preservation of The Red Knight."

They had fully discussed the scheme of launching the astounding fact of the discovered variety when Margaret Grant dashed into the glade with a shout and a clatter of hoofs.

"Greetings, kind friends!" she announced with a swagger. "Permit Flash, four-footed gentleman of the highroad, to join your sweet company with Gooseberry up."

"To horse!" cried Ned, catching the conceit of the girl. "To horse! We ride with the gallant Goose!"

"The very thing!" laughed Mary.

Riding close Margaret struck vengefully. But Ned dodged and assisting Mary into the saddle swung up on Darkey and the laughing cavalcade rode out of the glade.

From his covert Reddy Sykes saw them depart. Waiting until he was sure they were safely away he returned to his horse and mounting rode hastily back to Pellawa.

XII
ANYTHING IS FAIR IN LOVE...

The troop of three were retracing the course followed by Ned in his ride to the Glade. Trotting along the wet sand at the water's edge they had rounded the Pellawa end of the lake and were hugging the north shore, riding into the west at a spanking gait when Ned suddenly pulled Darkey and pointed up the sheer hill. A black speck was moving along the summit far above.

"Margaret! Behold!" was Ned's laughing shout.

The girls reined in abruptly and followed his hand.

"It is Andy!" cried Mary gaily. "I see where we lose our Gooseberry, promptly and automatically."

As she uttered the words a shout floated down from the silhouette above and the rider sent his mount over the bank. The brave brute took the precipice with a sure nonchalance, sliding on all fours or "sitting" the perpendicular slides with swift and perilous drop.

"Lucifer hits the toboggan!" cried Ned.

"The magnificent dare-devils!" exclaimed Mary, thrilled by the sight. In a moment it was over and Andy closed in upon them at a smart trot, reining his horse on his heels but a length before them.

"A mighty fine slide!" applauded Ned.

"Margaret can't peep," teased Mary. "Her heart's in her mouth."

Margaret acknowledged the newcomer with a sedate bow. Her voice was severely accusing as she said:

"Why do you find it necessary to skid that horrible hill on poor Night?"

"Just dropping into good company, Margaret," was the bright reply. "Night likes it."

"Very well! You are welcome to—the skidding," was the demure impertinence.

She turned from him to glance over the lake. Had Andy caught her eyes he would have seen deep down in their dark depths a gleam of exquisite pleasure. Good riding, and daring at that, could not fail to delight Margaret, and of this the wily Andy was well aware. A moment later he was enjoying her gay sallies as they rode side by side.

The four riders advanced abreast with the girls in the centre, the sound of their voices mingling with the champing of bits and the restless tramping of prancing hoofs. Suddenly, to their right, a gully opened up, winding its way into the hills. Andy caught Ned's eye flashing him some significant message. Ned instantly realized his intention and seizing Bobs' bridle turned abruptly into the gully. In the meantime Andy had adroitly directed Margaret's attention to a big loon basking in the water near the shore. They were well past the gully before she discovered that two of the party were missing. She halted Flash and looked blankly at Andy. With remarkable address he simulated her expression. She searched his nonplussed features critically, passing their fluctuations through her mental sieve.

"Two is company!" ejaculated Andy, shrugging his shoulders and looking back upon the empty trail.

"And three a crowd!" supplemented Margaret.

"And four a multitude!" completed Andy, a tone of satisfaction betraying him.

Margaret tipped her head a trifle haughtily and looked thoughtfully out over the lake.

"We have good company here, at any rate," ventured Andy.

Again Margaret gave him that searching glance. For a moment she studied him, then the glimmers of a whimsical mischief shone in her eyes and throwing back her head she laughed merrily.

"What transparent creatures you men are!" was her

99

naïve remark. "Obviously you and Ned arranged this sudden and innocent happening."

"How do you know?" challenged Andy boldly.

"How very like a man!" she cried, laughing quietly. "There you go confessing it. How do I know? Simply because Mary and I did not arrange it. It just happened. And Mary! I wonder. Was Mary kidnapped or is she an accomplice deep-dyed in guilt? Never mind. There's a loon on the water and two more on the shore. We'll go ahead to the Big Stone and wait for them."

So came Andy's opportunity, effected by his masterly strategy and the conniving Ned.

Their horses secured, they took seats in comfortable niches of the great stones and let their gaze sweep over the lake. A steady breeze fanned their faces and the water lapped musically about the base of the rock. It set Margaret musing.

"Do you hear it, Andy?" she cried. "I could stay here forever and dream of the sea. The sea is in my blood and— my heart,—always in my heart. I have but to shut my eyes and I am a wild, free Norse-girl tossing on the deep, or—a bold pirate."

"Pirate is better," said Andy with a grin. "You are always stealing something from me—secrets and other things. These dead Norse maidens appear to better advantage these days among the zoological collections of infamous old bones in famous old museums."

Margaret looked up severe and shocked.

"Thank you!" said she with dignity. "You have an affectionate regard for my ancient ancestors."

"None whatever!" retorted Andy. "Not a little bit. They are animals of another and stonier age. Give me a nice living girl with plenty of breath in her body and a soft heart,—one with a laugh in her eyes and her soul, who can loll comfortably on a rock and revel dreamily in sheer langour and laziness; a girl for instance like Margaret Grant."

"You don't like me when I'm poetic—rapt."

"Don't I? How like a woman! You want me to confess that I am mad about you. But I will not, for I am not—not the very slightest."

Margaret glanced up curiously, a smile playing about her lips.

"The fact is, Margaret," continued Andy, "I do like you —just you, in any mood, at any time and on any condition. It is not a foolish, mad regard; just a cool, composed, deliberate but fatal, tremendously fatal affection."

"Why fatal, Andy? I don't like the word."

"Take a look at me. Can you not see doom written all over me?"

Margaret looked. Their eyes met. She smiled whimsically.

"You look for all the world like a Norseman ready for Valhalla. But you are a very live and hopeful and preposterous Yellow-hair. In what way am I connected with this horrible doom?"

"You are the wild Norse girl that has demented your Norseman."

"Then you are mad after all?"

Again their eyes met. A unique confusion lay behind the light in the man's; something inscrutable behind the humorous banter in the girl's. Yet it was a happy unembarrassed moment. Andy seized it.

"Margaret," he said, rising and stepping toward her. "You guessed my artifice all right. I alone am to blame for

101

sending Ned and Mary up the gully. There was no plot, only on my part. I decided that we must come to a clear understanding. Lately I have had hours of anxious reflection. I wanted to see you alone to-day. Do you think you love me, Margaret?"

The girl turned frank, open eyes upon him, all levity gone. There was something looking out of his eyes that made her tremble. A deep seriousness stole over her face. Slowly she averted her gaze, looking out into the lake. For a long time she was silent. Then she said gently:

"I love no one else, Andy. But—I—I cannot answer your question. I know you love me. I am not sure that I love you. Do I love you? I—I cannot say. Perhaps I do. I have always thought I did. It may be true. It may all have come about in a way so gradual, so natural, so ordinary that I am confused. I cannot answer you—now. I do not know. Something will help us."

Looking up she met his eyes. They were full of trouble. A wave of compunction swept over her. Holding out her hands she leaned toward him.

"Come," she said simply, "you may kiss me, Andy. I love your kisses."

"How I would like to," was his quiet return as he fought the temptation. "But I cannot. It would not be right. You have a tender heart, Margaret. I love you ever so much more in the last few moments. I shall wait for the right to kiss you. Perhaps it will come."

The girl looked up surprised, a faint flush dyeing her face. Their attachment had obtained for years and since the engagement two years before they had enjoyed the sweet amenities of true lovers. A pang smote her as she realized that he was right.

Upon riding back they discovered the delinquent couple enjoying the shade of a giant oak just beyond the entrance to the gully. Joining forces the troop rode homeward.

XIII
THE RED KNIGHT SCORES

The air was full of the merry laughter of children. It was the hour of noon and Mary McClure was busy placing some afternoon work upon the blackboard. A sound on the porch caused her to hold her flying hand. In a little there was a rap at the door and a giant form stepped in.

"Good-day, lassie," said the deep voice of Ed. Pullar.

"Well, Mr. Pullar!" was the girl's cordial greeting as she turned toward him. "How glad I am to see you. Have you news of The Red Knight?"

The venerable face was wreathed in smiles. The happiness boded good tidings.

Bowing with cavalier grace he replied:

"Here is the communication. I want you to read it, lassie."

Stepping lightly to him she took the sheet and pored over it swiftly. Its contents were of extreme interest to her. It ran:

DEAR SIR:

Doubtless you have received my letter acknowledging the safe arrival of your packages of Red Knight. The tests are proceeding apace and already we are able to report results that may be of far-reaching import to the grain growers of the WORLD. They will assuredly be gratifying to you.

Your samples have been subjected to an exhaustive series of milling tests, disclosing the presence in Red Knight of ASTONISHING MILLING PROPERTIES.

Also, we have studied carefully your very complete history of the discovery and isolation of the new variety and find that throughout the germination tests up to the present stage, our observations have resulted in a remarkable parallel of your own record.

On the afternoon of the nineteenth we are holding a Staff Conference to consult on the phases of Red Knight, referred to above, with a view to consider the speeding up of test operations. The imminency of the ensuing seed-time demands this if we are to launch comprehensive field tests in ALL OUR NATIONAL FARMS.

At the close of the Conference an informal luncheon will be tendered to the DISCOVERERS of THE RED KNIGHT. We request the presence of yourself and your son as the honourable guests of the occasion.

I have the honour to be, sir,

Your obedient servant,
JOHN T. C. NORRGRENE,
Minister of Agriculture.

As she finished Mary clasped the letter to her breast, lost in a moment's pensiveness. Then she lifted to the earnest face above her eyes aglow with a brimming pleasure.

"You will go, Mr. Pullar!" she cried delightedly. "You will go, of course, both you and Ned."

"Yes, I will go," was the quiet reply. "I have no desire now to tramp abroad but I am going to do whatever I can to help these great men discover the true character of The Red Knight. Ned is coming with me. Dad Blackford will take care of the farm. It is a great moment for Ned and me."

The gray head lifted with a perceptible pride.

"Mr. Pullar!" she cried, stepping nearer to him. "Do I look pleased?"

He read the girl's face.

"Aye! It is so, lassie. 'Tis the bonny bit you have been with your bright, loyal heart."

"I am more than pleased," returned Mary. "I am elated. It means that your big, noble plans will be realized. There can be no hitch now. The Red Knight is doing splendid work alone, but when you and Ned join forces with him you will be irresistible. I see glorious times ahead."

The old man looked deep into the eyes bright with the magic of a great hope.

"Bonny Mary!" said he gently. "Bonny Mary!—that is what I have been calling you in my secret mind.—You have been a right wonderful blessing to me for you—you believe in me. And your beauty and tenderness they have been recalling the past these happy hours in the wee school-house. I cannot thank you——"

"Hush, Mr. Pullar!" was her gentle interruption. "You cannot thank people for their—their regard, for their—love. You—you just do it too. You love them back. Do you not?"

The naïve, girlish innocence touched him. Placing a great hand gently on her head he stooped down and brushed her brow ever so lightly with his lips.

"God bless you, lassie!" was the reverent benediction.

She watched him go out, his face beautiful with a new light.

On the edge of the clearing he halted and looked back to the school.

"Aye! God bless you, lassie!" was his whisper. "May He keep the light o' laughter always in your bonny eyes! Always!"

The proud form that vanished into the trees was not unlike the strong young Apollo who wooed the dainty Kitty Belaire. Old Ed. Pullar was putting up a fight, the stress of which was known to only two. Ned realized it by the insight of his great affection; and Mary by the tender intuition of her woman's heart.

XIV

BEHIND THE GREEN BAIZE DOOR

It was December, but the balm of the bright days belied the season. The fall had elongated into a second springhood and save for a crispness in the evening air it might have been April. Then, with the sudden vagary of prairie weather, came a change. It was three days after the reception of the invitation to the luncheon. The morning opened up with the mellow warmth of Indian summer. Ned Pullar and his father carried their light overcoats upon their arms as they boarded the seven-thirty for the long ride to the City. An hour later a chill breath swept down from the north and winter was on. Before their journey was half completed the yellow and black landscape had given place to a truly December white.

Winter assumed the reins of power by the grand inaugural of a considerable blizzard. The wind was not as riotous and gusty as in the dreaded storm but steady and cold, snowing heavily and driving a close, surface blow. Night drew down the curtain with the temperature slightly lower, the breeze unabated in its mild steadiness and the snow falling in a thickening sheet. With the stars blanketed by heavy clouds and the moon stark dead the night was black. The white covering of snow made little difference to the impenetrable pall.

Pellawa was unusually quiet though a few hardy pedestrians braved the deepening drifts. Louie Swale's joint, however, boasted a small and interesting crowd. About the bar were some familiar faces, Snoopy Bill Baird, Nick Ford and other members of McClure's Gang. The Green Baize Door was shut. Two men occupied the privacy of the "Square Room," sitting on opposite sides of the table, each with his amber-hued flask. Rob McClure was plainly on the defensive, withstanding some daring proposition being urged by Reddy Sykes. Their frequent swigs were beginning to undermine McClure's scepticism.

"You think this Red Knight wheat, as you call it, is no hoax," said Rob.

"It's the real goods," averred Sykes positively. "Pullar has tested it for four years and the experts in the University have pronounced it O.K. That is why Ned and the old man are toting into the City. It is good enough to be valued by Ned at one hundred dollars a bushel. They tell me John T. C. Norrgrene is interested in this thing himself. This wheat is due to cause a sensation with the result that Ned Pullar's stock goes up higher in the community as well as somewhere else. Ned Pullar's a mighty clever gink and I have a hunch that he has nothing on his old man. They've hit it lucky. The Red Knight is a gold mine to them."

McClure scowled.

"Grant that there's anything in it, how do you propose to get hold of the wheat? Four hundred bushels is a big thing to lift."

"Easy when you go about it right. I've got it whittled to a hair trigger. Touch it and away she comes. You want to clap your claws on Pullar. Here is your chance to sink 'em deep. That four hundred bushels of Red Knight means more to old Ed. Pullar than his farm, stock and the whole works. He's doting on it. That makes it mean still more to Ned.

Here is your chance to hand Pullar and Son a dizzy one."

Sykes paused a moment while he took a long drink. McClure pondered the proposition with a face that grew craftier the longer he simmered. His cogitations were suspended suddenly, however, by an innovation in the features of his companion. The pull of liquor had provoked immediate result, altering Sykes' countenance and causing a sudden expansion of his confidence. With his face overspread by a secretive leer he leaned closer and whispered:

"I haven't let it loose before, Rob, but I have red-hot grudge against your friend Pullar. That party has cut into my trail three or four times in as many years. We've locked horns before but the breaks went to him. His luck takes a sag to-night. There are three ways we can beat him up. We can get him through the old man in the way we've been figuring. This would cripple him for fair, but we've got to wait for our chance. It will come. The next best bet is a raid on The Red Knight. This thing is bigger than you are reckoning. Relieve him of this bunch of seed wheat and what have we done? We take forty thousand dollars out of his pocket and smother the one big howl of the old man's life. I am for putting over this surprise right off the bat."

He paused. McClure waited patiently.

"Go on," said Rob. "Give us your third bullet. It may do the trick alone. What is it?"

At the query Sykes' face changed in a manner that surprised even his hardened colleague. The unscrupulous plotter became a fiend repulsively malicious. From his eyes shot a jealous malignity, while upon every muscle of his face outcropped the pure depravity of hate. The mask had inadvertently slipped. Instinctively Sykes caught himself and replaced it. As McClure continued to search his face he realized that his companion was wearing his usual inscrutable smile. He could scarcely believe that the fiendish thing had disclosed itself.

"Never mind number three," said Sykes. "This is not a good time to consider it. It will be useful later."

McClure looked at him askance. The fellow possessed a knowledge that baffled him. A vague uneasiness crept into his mind, a premonition warning him of the man. Sykes realized that he had jeopardized matters not a little and exercised all his congenial graces to destroy the effect on the mind of his companion. He turned adroitly to levity and the flask and very soon they were on the old footing of boon companionship.

"We must get hold of The Red Knight," said McClure, swinging suddenly in line under the spell of the odorous whiskey. "And the sooner, the better."

"To-night!" announced Sykes with a fierce shutting of his jaws.

McClure looked surprised.

"It's blowing a blizzard," was his objection. "And it's a good ten mile run."

"The kind of night I should select to kill a man," returned the other. "I could slip up to him out of the storm, pass him out and drop into the blizzard again. The snow would obligingly cover all trails. It is now eight o'clock. Bill Baird and his men are ready, six teams all told. They will pull the little raid at twelve. Each man will have a sleigh with double box and no bells. They will slip up the Valley along Pullar's hay trail to his barnyard, coming in from the field instead of the road. The wheat is all located—two hundred bushels in the house, a hundred in the granary

110

and the balance in a portable bin in the southeast quarter."

"But Blackford is at the house. He'll put up a scrap. You can't pull Dad's leg. He'll make a mess of it."

"We've arranged to put the old bloke away while the fun is on and it won't need any rough work. Leave Blackford to me."

"But they'll drop on us instantly without a clue. They'll search my farm and the elevators and every building in Pellawa."

Sykes threw back his head in glee.

"You're late coming into the game, Rob. That's the trouble!" And he poked the other playfully on the chest. "We are not bringing the wheat in here. Oh, no. There is Old Hunt's, the Squatter's shack. It is water tight and drift tight and has not been used since the old geezer kicked out two years ago. The boys will drop the stuff there and we can market it by degrees through the winter. We'll hush up the detective stunt with an alibi, an alibi that will cover the honour of eight good men. Here's the how. The gang's with Louie now. When we are ready they come in here for an all-night deal. Louie and the crowd see them enter. We let them out quietly through the rear into the dark. They sneak through the snow and do the job and turn up here in the wee sma' hours. Louie will not disturb the Square Room. But he can swear that we held it for the night. We'll make it worth his while. There you are. But the alibi will not be needed at all. The blizzard will blind the trail and pad the whole event. This storm will cover over any track in ten minutes. It is getting late and the men are waiting."

Sykes paused significantly.

"Call them in," said McClure, rubbing his hands in glee. "You are a wonder, Red! We'll send them on the smart hike."

The Green Baize Door opened and closed a few minutes later on the full gang of plotters. After being put through a detailed rehearsal of Sykes' plan they drank a copious draft to the success of the adventure.

"This will be a come-back on that blankety Hallowe'en foul," said Snoopy Bill with an avenging grin. "We'll proceed to tap Pullar a little for his fun."

The remark was followed by a chorus of curses that revealed the rankle of revenge. This motive was the sleeping thing Sykes had roused in his plying of the gang.

"You'll reach Pullar's farm around twelve," concluded Sykes. "A half-hour should see you loaded for the haul to Hunt's. You'll be back here by four. Come in quietly."

Thus adjured, Snoopy Bill and his men, stealing out through the rear, vanished into the darkness and set off on their expedition.

XV
ONE BLACK NIGHT

Dad Blackford was late in doing up the chores, for the snow had presented him with some unforeseen problems, hampering greatly the bedding and feeding. Not until everything was snug from the storm did he think of indulging in his evening solace. While dreaming amid the blue circles of smoke there came to him Ned's admonition about The Red Knight. It was his last word.

"See that no harm comes to The Red Knight, Dad," was Ned's laughing caution. "It is the one thing on the farm that

Dad would not part with."

"Ah!" said the old man with sudden decision, "I maun take a turn hout to the barn. The snow moight 'arm the bonny corn."

Lighting his lantern he went out and was gratified to find that the grain was snugly secure. When he came in he went to the room where lay the two hundred bushels. Opening the door he flashed his lantern about. Here, too, all was weather-tight. At sight of the pile of wonderful wheat he exclaimed in admiration. Picking up a handful he held it close to the light.

"'Ee's wealthy-loike!" said the old man, caressing the plump brown grains with his fingers. "'Ee's the fat corn und 'evvy! The old un'll make a pile on un."

Shutting the door he returned to his pipe and dreamed of visions of riches in store for Ned and his father, his innocent old face glowing with pleasure at the contemplation of their good fortune. Rising at length he went to the door, took a long look out into the black night, then shut it carefully and retired to his bed.

It was nearing the hour of midnight when he was aroused from sleep by a thumping upon the door. Rising he threw up the sash and looked down.

"Hello! Is that Mr. Blackford?" called an anxious voice.

"Hit be," was the succinct response.

"I am from Jake McCarragh's. One of his mares is down and he wants you to come over and give us a hand."

"Ah! 'Ee's a 'orse sick. Ah'll coome along," was the kind response.

"I'm on the hike," said the voice below. "I'll foot it back on the double quick and help Jake. You hurry after as fast as you can."

The case was evidently urgent.

"Hal roight, go a'ead. Ah'll be along," replied the old man, hastening to dress.

In a short time he was ready and stepped out into the storm, trudging down the lane and off into the north with the blizzard in his face. He did not hear the muffled beat of galloping hoofs as he emerged into the road-allowance.

As we have mentioned before, there were pedestrians about the drifted streets of Pellawa. One of these venturesome wanderers was the little French bagger of the Valley Outfit, Jean Benoit. He had come to Pellawa in the morning and untoward obstructions had kept him from setting out on his return home. He was still "hung up" and was plunging impatiently through the drifts with determination to make a swift wind up of business when he heard a voice down the lane to his right.

"You are sure Pullar's away?" came clearly through the storm.

"Went in on the morning train with the old man," replied another voice.

Jean halted. The mention of Pullar had awakened his curiosity.

"I'd hate to run into the Valley boss. He's a bang-up hitter."

"No danger. We're squaring with Pullar to-night. He'll never know who pinched his wheat."

At this point a mutual laugh came through the darkness.

"You meet me with the others at Morrison's bluff. That's the line, eh?"

"Righto! We'll slip into Pullar's yard about twelve. So long."

There was no more. The men had passed on. Jean lingered. He had not caught the full significance of the brief dialogue, for he could not hear every word and the English troubled him in places. He pieced enough together, however, to conclude that some foul work was meditated against Ned. He held his counsel and rushed through preparations for departure. As he took the South Cut in his descent into the Valley he saw a light in the Grant home. So agitated had he become in his review of the incident in the village that he decided to lay the matter before Charles Grant.

The farmer was in bed, but at his knock a light step tripped down the stairs and Margaret opened the door. She invited him in. Grant was promptly aroused and evidenced serious perturbation at Jean's story.

"I am afraid there is some devilment afoot," was his comment. "You say there may be a big gang at work?"

"Wan, two, tree, four! Mebbe other! I do not know. I tink many."

"Can it be an attempt to steal Mr. Pullar's new wheat?" ventured Margaret. "Mary has been telling me so much about it. I saw her to-day. Ned and his father have gone into the City at the call of John T. C. Norrgrene."

"It may be that, lass," agreed her father. "Jean's tale points that way."

"They are after The Red Knight!" said Margaret with intuitive conviction. "It is a terrible night. What can poor old Dad Blackford do against a gang of daring thieves?"

"We'll take a hand in it ourselves," said Grant grimly. "Jean, you take the south trail and let Easy Murphy know. I'll dress and pick up Lawrie and——"

115

"I'll saddle Flash, Dad," interrupted Margaret. "I'm all ready. I can ride over and let Andy know."

Grant looked at the girl a second, considering.

"Very well, lass! Do it," said her father with a smile. "Ye're good for it and there is not any time to waste. Be careful, for the night is dark."

Before her father had reached the stable Margaret was in the saddle and away.

Andy was easily aroused and in an incredibly short time was astride Night.

"You ride back home," directed he to Margaret. "I'll push Night through. It is half-past eleven and we have four miles to run. I may be in time to scare them off. Your Dad and the others will be right on my heels."

With a farewell shout he plunged into the storm. The sound of Night's speeding hoofs smote her ears then died away. Reluctantly she turned Flash for home and trotted off. They had proceeded but a few rods when she reined him in and halted abruptly, loitering irresolute.

"Come, Flash! About!" was her sudden command. "We'll be in it, too."

Wheeling her mount she sent him at a gallop after Night and his rider.

Andy put his horse through at a stiff pace. The homestead was shrouded in blackness as he approached. Riding through the gate he cantered swiftly down the lane, and pulled up beside the house. He had but halted when he discerned the dim movement of figures on all sides of him. With the consciousness of their presence came the realization that they were men.

116

"Good-night, gentlemen!" he called.

But there was no reply. Instead he could hear smothered cries of chagrin and savage anger, followed by a rush of the encompassing forms. Night's bridle was seized and strong hands grappled him, dragging him from the saddle. Terrified by the rough handling and mysterious commotion the horse reared and plunged, tearing away from her captors. Leaping free she dashed off down the lane.

As Andy came to earth he clutched one of his assailants and they rolled over. In the darkness the others seizing his foeman by mistake wrenched him away, leaving Andy free. Leaping to his feet, he backed to the wall of the house. Discovering their mistake they rushed him again. He struck out and a shadow staggered and fell. They closed in as another went down. Hands seized him on every side. He was struggling mightily, tossing his assailants about, when he heard a voice shrill out above the smothered tumult. He realized that it was Margaret's cry and conscious that help was near, fought with renewed fury to free his arms. Then something crashed upon his head and he tottered back, falling in a heap against the wall.

Speeding along on the trail behind, Margaret had not spared her horse. She had slowed up and was peering through the darkness for the gate when Flash swerved violently, almost unseating her. At the same time there dashed past her some fleeing thing. All she caught was the dim shadow of an empty saddle and flying stirrups. She knew it was Night. Thrilled by a foreboding of disaster she charged down the lane. She rode up to the house, halting Flash on his haunches at the group of struggling men. She could hear the heavy breathing and knew that Andy was fighting desperately with his back to the wall. She thought of riding Flash upon them but checked him, fearing she might injure Andy himself. A sense of impotence swept over her. Then flashed into her mind an idea. Rising in her stirrups she shouted:

"Father! Men! This way!"

Immediately Andy went down, but at the same instant Snoopy Bill and his men were stampeded. Sure that a rescue party was on them they dropped their victim and bolted for the sleighs. Leaping in they whirled their teams about and lashing them to a run fled out of the yard and back over the fields.

Ten minutes later when Grant galloped up with the others they found Margaret sitting in the snow with Andy's head upon her lap.

"Lassie!" cried the astonished Grant. "You here?"

"Yes, Father!" was her quiet reply. "I got here too late to save Andy. They've hurt him terribly."

"Be easy, lass!" soothed the man, "it may not be sae serious. The lad will be coming round in a meenit."

They carried him into the house and laid him upon a couch. A quick examination discovered a gash in the head from some heavy implement.

"It is a concussion," said Grant. "But not vera deep. Aye, he is coming out."

Andy opened his eyes. The first object he became conscious of was the face of Margaret bending over him. Smiling faintly he observed in surprise:

"You here, Margaret? I thought I heard you shout just before they got me."

He closed his eyes drowsily.

"You sent me home," she whispered in his ear. "But I changed my mind and followed you."

When she looked up she discovered that they were alone.

"You should not have come," was the gentle reprimand.

"Indeed? I think you were very rude to send me away."

"But I am glad you are here, now," said he contentedly.

"You really are?"

"Really."

"And so am I," said the girl softly. "Because—because, Andy, that wonderful 'something' has happened. Now I know beyond all doubt that I have always loved you and—I love you now."

"Then," said he, drawing her head down to him, "then — —"

"You may kiss me with a clear conscience, Andy."

While Margaret was dispensing her welcome ministrations Grant and his men were going over the buildings. Their swift search found everything intact. Two of the riders who had gone out to the portable granary reported all well there. Not a grain of The Red Knight had been touched. While this was gratifying, the men's faces were exceedingly grave. Nowhere on the premises could they find Dad Blackford. They were beginning to discuss the probability of foul play when Easy Murphy gave a yell.

"Hist, ladies and gintlemen!" said he. "Take a look. 'Tis the missing link himsilf, disguised as Santa Clause."

They all took a look and there on the porch stood Dad Blackford hatless and dishevelled, with snow-matted beard and a very red and perspiring face. He was blowing like a grampus and looked for all the world like the merry personality of Christmas tide. His eyes were astonished at the sight they met and how they sparkled as they recounted to him the night's adventures. His joy at finding that all was well more than compensated for the shameless treatment he had received at the hands of the artful Sykes.

When Margaret got him alone she somewhat surprised him.

"Never mind, Dad," she confided. "After all it's been a delightful adventure. Andy got a sore head but it will soon be better. His heart is well again."

Dad looked at her a moment dumbfounded. Then he tumbled and the laughter of a merry heart twinkled in his eyes.

"Been 'avin' a quarrel with un?" he teased.

"No. Just a little misunderstanding," she whispered back.

This bit of confidence turned the whole affair into a thing of joy for the kind-hearted old Englishman.

While this tête-à-tête was taking place the men were riding down the vandals by the aid of lighted lanterns. The trail was dim to begin with, however, and grew dimmer as they swerved to the west out upon the high prairie. Here it vanished altogether and the party returned. The blackness of the night and the heavily drifting snow enabled Snoopy Bill and his men to make a clean get-away.

Following Sykes' plan providing for misadventure they turned into the west instead of the east and recrossed the Valley about the west end of the lake, eventually arriving in the Square Room thoroughly wearied and disgruntled and two hours behind schedule time.

Sykes' face was a picture of blank dismay; McClure's of

rage.

"Where is the squealer?" cried Bob McClure as he stalked among the men.

Blasphemous and resentful protestations quite evidently sincere came from all parts of the room.

"No, Rob!" said Snoopy Bill deliberately. "You are a liar if you say it. There isn't a squealer in the gang. Not a man laid down. Any squealing that may have taken place was let out by the gents who stayed behind."

Reddy Sykes read the savage light in Baird's eyes.

"You are straight, Bill," he cried soothingly. "Straight as a die and I know it. The boys came through. But somebody outside got wise. We'll find out and when we do somebody's due to get a blankety unpleasant surprise. The whole thing ran out to dope. We should have that wheat in Hunt's shack. It's Pullar's luck. But it will change. Here's to a lucky break."

He held his flask high. The men caught his spirit and responded with a shout. For an hour the crew caroused, drinking heavily as they debated the fiasco, breaking up before dawn.

Dad Blackford made a full report to Ned. Though no trace of the perpetrators of the offense had been obtained, his mind flew instantly to his two enemies. The Red Knight had been their objective. The incident was big with warning to him. It assured him of two things: of their malicious, untiring hate; of their dangerous resource. Thoughts of Mary pressed heavily upon him. He remembered her words:

"There is no other way. But, Ned, you will have to be right, always, as well as irresistible. I know you will be."

"It's a stiff programme, little girl," he reflected ruefully. "But we'll stay with it."

XVI

THE SPIDER WEAVES

Snow! Snow! In glistening deserts! Ghastly white blankets of it hung to the sky-rim! The hills, frosted bridal cakes, terrace on terrace! The valleys, rolls and folds and gouges of white! Over all the blue yawn of an empty sky! The air stabs with its invisible, minute Damascus daggers. It is a smiting vacuity, frozen, tense. One's breath floats from the lips in a powdered cloud of whitening mist. It is winter—the snapping, crackling, detonating, hoary-headed winter of the North!

The February sun pours down on the plains in a fierce, garish flow, shedding no warmth from its low-slanting shafts. Pellawa is hushed to sepulchral solitude in the grim embrace of "forty below." An occasional sleigh drifts phantom-like along the street, its runners emitting a frosty singing. Only the dozens of smoke columns rising straight and high in the air proclaim the village a haunt of the living.

Wrapped in the comfort of an immense buffalo coat, Reddy Sykes stepped into a waiting cutter.

"Rob McClure's!" was his brief direction to the driver.

As the team trotted down the street and out over the white expanse he settled himself snugly among the robes. Sykes was in fine fettle, with eyes unusually bright. His great chest expanded in deep breaths of self-gratification. His elation was somewhat due to the bibber's effervescence. The odour of his habitual elixir exhaled copiously from his breath. But here was another stimulant none the less powerful. The fox was out with his nose in the wind hugging a live trace. There was game in the wind.

He reached McClure's as the sun rolled under the reddened valley in a disk of blood. Leaving the cutter he stepped briskly to the door. While stamping the snow from his feet, preparatory to knocking, a musical voice greeted him and Mary McClure appeared miraculously at his side, an apple-cheeked, cherry-lipped Venus-in-furs. She had just driven in from The Craggs.

"Pardon me!" said Sykes, in cavalier attentiveness, reaching out for the knob she had already taken. The rare beauty of the girl and her close presence ensnared him. Recklessly obedient to a sudden impulse, he seized her hand and drew her closer to him. For the briefest instant he looked into her eyes with daring assurance.

"Mary!" he said softly, imprisoning firmly her struggling hand, "what a chic little wench you are! Do you realize that you are maddening in those furs, with your eyes and colour and lips? Your lips!" he repeated, leaning toward her.

The cordial smile faded swiftly from her eyes and the red cheeks blanched.

"Please release my hand, Mr. Sykes," she commanded, in a low, distressed tone.

Looking down into her indignant eyes he saw something there that counselled hasty obedience. He let go at once.

"Sorry, Mary!" was his apology in a tone affecting deep penitence. "I am demented over you. You are distracting to-night. Will you let me in? I have come to see your father."

Making no reply she opened the door.

"Mr. Sykes is here, Mother," was the quiet announcement. "He drove up just as I came in from stabling Bobs. He wishes to see Father at once."

Mrs. McClure cordially welcomed the effusively agreeable guest, guiding him to the office. In a very few minutes he reappeared, accompanied by McClure, who proceeded to make hasty preparations for the trail.

"You go ahead," said he to Sykes. "I'll come along in my own rig."

"Are you leaving before tea?" asked Mrs. McClure in surprise.

"Yes," was the abrupt response. "We have a big deal on. I'll not be back until late."

As the men went out the two women looked at each other in silent significance. On the topic of father and husband their lips were sealed. At the moment their minds were exceedingly busy. The burning light in Mary's eyes disturbed her mother.

"You are troubled, daughter?" was the gentle question as she threw her arms about the girl. "Perhaps it will help us both to talk it over. I think it high time that we should resume our little confidences."

Returning the embrace and caress, Mary looked soberly into her mother's eyes.

"It is a fear I have had for weeks, Mother," said she, responding to her mother's question. "Until to-day it was more or less vague. Now it is real. I am convinced there is ground for a little anxiety on my part. Can you not surmise it?"

Helen McClure studied the serious eyes so near her. She shook her head.

"No. I do not think it would be wise to guess. Can you not tell me?"

"I shudder at the influence Mr. Sykes has over Father," said Mary reminiscently. "It alarms me to see that power grow stronger every day. Candidly, Mother, I am afraid of the deal they are in such haste to arrange. There was something unpleasantly secretive in their manner just now. I did not like the look in Dad's eyes."

"Is this your fear?" pressed the mother gently.

"This is involved," returned Mary. "I have an even more personal anxiety. I am afraid of the man, Chesley Sykes. He is growing too attentive and familiar. Why? I do not know. I have never liked him and he has no right to press his intimacy. He is irrepressible, laughs at my snubs and deports himself with such annoying confidence. This all came about suddenly in the early winter. Why should he insist on a friendship that is detestable to me?"

Mary paused, awaiting some response to her appeal. But her mother hazarded no guess.

"You will remember, Mother," resumed Mary reflectively, "that I stopped riding the Valley during those wonderful days in December. I did that because of a wholesome fear of Chesley Sykes. I had a persistent feeling that he was shadowing me. Several times during my rides along the river I 'happened' upon him. One day, seized with an intuition that somebody was trailing me, I slipped into a cowpath and detouring quickly, watched the back trail from a covert. In a few minutes Sykes rode up on that big hunter of his. He pulled up at the cowpath and leaning down studied it a moment. Satisfied, at length, he turned into Bobs' tracks and followed me. As he turned down the path he spoke to his horse. I caught the words and they frightened me.

"'King!' said he, with that confident laugh, 'nothing our little lady can do will blind our trail. She'll find one Sykes in at the killing. She's a neat little fox but we'll gather her brush.'

"I shook him by sending Bobs into the Willow and up-stream. After riding out of sight about a bend we stole into the trees and made all haste for home.

"To-night at the door he was rude and maudlin. He had been drinking and was therefore unwise. He professed to be penitent, yet I could see his audacious assurance cropping out. This is the thing that makes me tremble. He has some reason for this boldness. He has Dad's approval. It is evidently Dad's will that I foster intimate relations with his friend. That I will not do."

Looking into her daughter's glowing eyes, Helen McClure was deeply conscious of the trouble there. Her own mind was alarmed and had been for many days. She knew only too well that Mary had plumbed correctly her father's intentions as to her relations with Sykes. She was also sure of something that the girl was only dimly suspicious of. She had long since concluded that the two men had reached some definite agreement that had far-reaching interest for Mary. Their projects seemed to involve her compliance. The mother knew that circumstances were leading to a clash of wills. But she decided that reticence was best for the present.

"I am sorry you are in trouble, Mary," said the mother affectionately. "You have certainly real ground for your distrust of Sykes. Avoid him. And if a swift decision should ever be thrust upon you, follow your heart. That is the only safe way. But we must not grow pessimistic, daughter. There are bright days ahead. We will help them to come quickly."

The reserve with which her mother spoke convinced Mary of grave reasons for caution. Running up to her room she pondered the events of the last hour. As she dwelt upon her experiences and pieced her disturbing reflections she found herself looking into the future with a distinct sense of trepidation.

The night was dark, a night of stars dazzlingly bright. There was a traveller on the Pellawa trail. Ned Pullar was drawing near the homestead upon his return from the village. The air was calm save for the slight drift of a five-mile breeze caused by his ride into the north. Even this faint wind had the biting tang of the extremely low temperature, forcing him to avert his face from its freezing breath. Giving a sudden, piercing whistle he sent his horses into a smart trot.

He was the prey to a vague uneasiness. That morning he had set out with his father with their two loads of Red Knight. A great deal of time had been spent at the village making up the shipments to the various national farms. It was late before they were ready to set out for home. Then occurred a hitch. They were taking back with them a power fanning mill. When they drove up to Nick Ford's implement shed they were disappointed to find that the mill had not been completely set up. It would take quite half an hour, so Ford advised them.

"I'll take the engine with me," said Ned. "I can set out ahead and get busy with the chores. You will be along in an hour or so."

"That will be the best plan," agreed the old man.

His father had no sooner agreed to the suggestion than a misgiving swept over Ned. A glance at his father's face reassured him, however, and he let the arrangement stand.

Loading the gasoline engine he set off. As he drove along he debated the wisdom of his decision. Three months ago he would not have left his father alone in Pellawa. But these months had seen a remarkable change in Edward Pullar. He had developed a dignity and self-reliance that Ned knew was based in a sudden accretion of strength. His dreams of The Red Knight were ennobling and the achievement of the hopes of long years had rallied him. He felt it safe to trust him alone in the village with its lurking danger, and yet— he wished again and again that he had waited with his father. The nearer he drew to the homestead the greater grew his uneasiness.

Edward Pullar went into the little office occupying a corner of the implement shed and sat down prepared to patiently await the completion of Ford's task. It was the only place in the village where he could pass the time with safety. Louie Swale's and Sparrow's both occurred to him as the common rendezvous of travellers, but he passed them up with a shudder. He well knew his weakness and wished greatly to vindicate Ned's faith in him. The business of setting up the mill did not progress continuously. In fact, several times Ford had dropped his tools to visit the Square Room. There he at length met Sykes and McClure. The trio held ominous consultation.

"Old Ed. is in my office," replied Ford to a question from Sykes. "Ned must be nearly home. You did not meet him?"

"No. He slipped down into the Valley just as we drove out of Rob's."

"I've killed about all the time I dare without arousing his suspicion. Let us get him in here."

McClure shook his head emphatically.

"Nothing doing," was his impatient retort. "He's dodged

it for months. We'll have to get him without his knowing it."

Sykes sat back watching the others and sipping his glass reflectively. With a laugh of easy assurance he rocked forward in his chair.

"It will be easy," said he with a cryptic smile. "It all depends on you, Ford. If you will take your time and keep your head the thing is done. I've got the paper ready. Old Ed. can hold a tankful and walk as straight as a post. I've seen him drunk as a lord but to all appearances as quiet and wise as a judge. We'll get Cy Marshall in to witness the deal. Cy's eyesight is not what it used to be, but it is all we could desire. Might be lucky later to have the documents OK-ed by a magistrate whose record is without blemish. Here is a little secret," said he, drawing a small vial from his pocket.

Opening the tube he dropped a tiny tablet into his palm. Glancing significantly at Ford he said:

"You are the only one who can use it, Nick."

But Ford shook his head dubiously.

"Perfectly harmless!" urged Sykes. "He'll sleep it down in six hours and—it gets you a couple of hundred now and a share when Foyle comes through."

Ford shifted. Sykes took out a roll of bills. While Ford hung back Sykes opened a flask and dropped in the tablet. The drug dissolved swiftly, leaving the liquor as before. Sykes laughed.

"I repeat, it is perfectly harmless," said he. "I could drink it myself." Then he added with a fiendish glimmer in his eyes Rob McClure had seen there once before, "They got you sloppy drunk last fall, Nick, and put Rob's gang on the hog, then threw you into the lake to cool you off. Here is your chance to hand Pullar a sleeper. Are you afraid to put this easy thing across?"

With a vengeful laugh Nick reached for the flask.

"See what we can do with it," said he grimly. "The laugh's on Ned."

"Rob and I'll meander down to the office," said Sykes casually. "We'll camp there for an hour. Cy is handy any time we want him. I'll stay at the desk. Rob will keep his eye on you and Old Ed. We'll have to work fast, but without any hurry, remember that, without any hurry while Cy is around."

Thrusting the flask in an inner pocket Ford took his departure.

Meanwhile Edward Pullar waited in the implement office. The room was very small and warmed by a very large air-tight heater. He grew so warm he took off his fur coat. Ford passed in and out, spending a moment in pleasant chat. Alone once more his inactivity and the warmth combined to make him drowsy. His head dropped forward at times in a brief doze. But he would instantly rouse and glance out the window. His throat and lips grew dry and a thirst came over him. He went over to a pail in the corner, but was disappointed to find it contained no water. He resumed his chair.

As he sat by the window looking out into the falling night Ford entered and after shuffling a moment about the little desk went out. The thirst recurred, but as there was no way to slake it, he patiently endured the discomfort. His thoughts followed Ned along the trail or drifted into the fascinating world of The Red Knight. Then the "thing" began to creep upon him. Gradually he became aware of an odour familiar and bibulously gratifying. At first it was but a fleeting inhalation. Then it became continuous, tripling in

130

its pleasing gratefulness. A possibility flashed into his mind. He glanced about. There it was upon the desk within easy reach. He could just discern it in the dim light. It was a flask three parts full. Ford had left it carelessly on the edge of the drop leaf, the cork out. Without any act of volition his hand reached out and his fingers closed on the glass. As he felt the dear, familiar form of the flask a mighty thirst welled up. But he halted, and, letting go of the bottle, snatched his hand away as if stung by a serpent. The realization of what he was about to do shook him strangely. Clenching his hands he turned away, lifting his head in proud resolution. He would fight this devil sitting so quietly by him.

Ford came in again and lit the dirty lamp. He picked up the bottle.

"You'll excuse me, Ed.," said he apologetically. "But it's so raw out there I've got to take a warmer. Just a nip. There!"

He had tipped the glass, but none of the liquor had passed his lips. The gurgle was maddening to the old man.

"You're welcome to a swig, Ed.," said Ford in a friendly manner. "But I'll not ask you to indulge, for I know you're on the water-wagon these days. I'll leave the 'wee drap' handy in case you take a notion."

He went out.

Ten minutes passed and the fight against the heat and the terrible thirst went swayingly on. The sight of the yellow liquid coupled with the subtle and odorous fumes from the breath of Bacchus plied him with an exquisite torment. He began to fear the "thing" again. Rising, he put on his coat and prepared for a stroll in the keen night without. With his hand on the door-knob he looked back, pausing irresolute. Slowly his fingers relaxed and he sat

131

down once more.

A physical lassitude began to steal over him, due to the excessive heat. The desire to drink became overmasteringly insistent. The smell of the vaporizing whiskey was sweeter than perfumes of Arabia. In a little he became conscious of nothing else. Then he found himself sitting beside the desk, leaning heavily upon it, the empty flask in his hand. His throat was parched and his brain on fire. He looked at the bottle with burning eyes. It was empty! Empty! As he contemplated it wildly Ford entered.

"Your mill is about ready," said he. "How are you making it?"

"Say, Nick!" whispered the old man cunningly, "I've stolen a march on you. The whiskey's all gone. I'd give a hundred dollars for a right good drink. Where can we get it?"

Ford looked at the inebriate, startled at the wild leer and the pitiable obsequiousness of the great figure.

"Too bad she's dry!" was the response. "That was the last drop I had. Come along with me. I'll fix you up."

They went out together, arriving a few minutes later at Sykes' office. Before they entered Ford whispered in his ear:

"Straighten up, Ed. That was strong stuff. It's got you swinging. These fellows will let you have all you want after you sign up."

"How?—how is that?" cried the old man in a half-startled voice, as he forced himself to walk erect.

"Hush!" was the admonitory reply. "It's this way. They have no right to let you have it, and unless you sign three or four little papers, promising not to give them away, why, of course, they don't take the chance. You do the signing and leave the rest to me. Keep straight while we are inside.

We'll get a bottle and go back to the shed."

"I understand, Nick," was the solemn response. "I'll protect the boys."

They entered. McClure, Sykes and Cy Marshall were within.

"Here is Ed. Pullar," said Nick. "He's ready to sign up and in an all-fired hurry. It's a long trip to The Craggs."

"We'll let him go quick," responded Sykes in a businesslike tone. "You sign here, Mr. Pullar."

Exerting all his power of will Edward Pullar wrote his name on a number of papers. The signature was duly certified by Cy Marshall. They loitered a moment, during which Sykes kept up a casual chat. Stepping near, Ford at length whispered:

"We'll get out. I've got it. Steady and slow, old man."

Obediently the old man followed him through the door. As the door shut his fingers closed around the promised flask. Then with a drunken punctiliousness he halted.

"Say, Nick!" was the shocked whisper. "We forgot to settle with the boys!"

Nick laughed.

"It's all right, Ed.," was the soothing response. "I laid down the price. It's my treat."

With a relieved laugh the old man trudged after him.

Ford assisted his victim to hitch up his horses and load the mill, joining him in a last drink before he sent him into the bitter night.

At his office Sykes sat back in his chair rubbing his hands complacently, while Rob McClure stared at the parchments decorated with the clear signature of Edward Pullar.

"It's a tidy little clean-up," was Rob's gratified

observation.

"Tidy's the word and tight!" agreed Sykes with acquiescing nods. "We've got Pullar hogtied with a two-inch rope. The law isn't made that can bust these agreements. When Hank Foyle signs up we wind up a very pleasant and totally regular deal."

Arrived at the homestead, Ned worked swiftly at his tasks. The chores finished, he ran into the house and busied himself preparing their simple meal. This too accomplished, he opened the mail and delved into the pile of letters. He had barely entered upon the perusal of the first letter when he set it down absent-mindedly. He was troubled at the non-appearance of his father. The uneasiness aroused along the trail changed suddenly to a fear that all was not right. He had expected to hear the bells within an hour after his arrival. It was now nearly two. Throwing on cap and coat, he walked down the lane to the road-allowance and peered into the main trail. It was empty as far as the eye could define. With hand to ear he listened. There was no sound in all the frozen stillness. It was a deadly night for the helpless traveller. The temperature was creeping lower every minute. He thought of the white death that steals noiselessly through a night like this. With the thought came a premonition. A depressive fear weighed him down.

Hurrying back to the house he made ready for a drive, leaving the waiting meal untouched. Throwing the driving harness on Darkey and his mate he hitched them to the cutter and set off for the village. They sped along at a twelve-mile clip, their nimble hoofs tattooing the dash with a fusillade of snow chips. The wind of their own motion smote his face with its subtle sting, blanching its exposed surfaces before he realized the frost was at work. Ducking into the warm collar, he avoided a bad bite. Crouching behind the wall of fur, his mind swiftly conjured the fate of an unfortunate numbed by the fancied warmth of liquor. Pathetic cases of terrible exposures and death flitted before his mind. Scarcely aware of it, he urged his flying horses to fifteen miles.

Unceasingly he searched the shadowy twin-ribbon of trail beyond the end of the cutter tongue. At length they dipped into the Northwest Cut and dashed over the Valley to the south climb. There as they were taking the sharp curve about a shoulder of the hill, his horses swerved suddenly in a shying leap. He halted them perilously near the edge of the steep embankment. Coming slowly about the hill was his father's team. They were taking the decline soberly and carefully and apparently on their own initiative. There was no driver in sight. At a sharp command from Ned they halted. Leaping from his cutter, he looked over the edge of the double box. In the bottom of the sleigh lay his father, motionless.

With a poignant cry Ned vaulted into the sleigh. He was shocked with a horrible fear as he discovered cap and gauntlets removed and coat wide open. A quick glance filled him with increased alarm. Hands and face of the sleeper were white with the wax-like colour of the dead. Hastily he thrust on cap and gauntlets and closed the open coat. Arranging the robes in the cutter, he carried the drunken form to the vehicle and placed it upon the seat. Taking the robes and even the empty bags out of the sleigh, he wrapped them about his father and took his place beside him. Whirling his frost-coated drivers about, he sent them furiously down the hill, leaving the heavy team to follow at their own sedate pace.

He did not spare the willing brutes ahead and pulled them up at the door in a cloud of steam. Throwing the robes upon them, he carried his father in and laid him upon the floor. Rushing out, he brought in pails of snow and set to work massaging the frozen face and hands. Circulation once more established, he carried the still inert form to his bed. This accomplished, he went out to his team and stabled them. The dumb brutes wondered at the swift tenderness with which he groomed away the thick coat of frost.

"You are not hurt a whit," said he gratefully, as he watched them happily munching their oats. "And you saved Dad."

The gentle taps with which he bid them good-night were comforting to their faithful equine spirits.

Out into the darkness he stepped, missing with a sudden and strange acuteness the mute sympathy of the animals now shut in the stables. The night was colder than ever and breathless with the hush of the lowering temperature. The silence of the farmstead depressed him. He looked at the house. It was a mysterious shape in the darkness, sheltering within it the wreck so pitiably still. Entering, he sat down to his long vigil. It was a lonely night for Ned Pullar—the loneliest he had ever known.

XVII
HANK FOYLE, UNEXPECTED GUEST

Three weeks later Edward Pullar was sitting up for the first time since his unfortunate visit to Pellawa. The scars of his terrible exposure were losing their virulence and strength was creeping back into the emaciated limbs.

No conversation touching the lamentable adventure had taken place. Once only had the father referred to it in broken and pathetic apology that was instantly hushed by the son. With the gentle assiduity of a mother Ned had nursed his patient and nobody in the settlement was aware of the disgrace of Edward Pullar, or of his narrow escape from the White Death of the northern trails.

For Ned, the lapse was after all only one in many. It was the latest, only a little more disappointing, more unfortunate and with the addition of tragedy barely avoided. To the father it was all this and more, infinitely more. There was a fear at his heart. He was penitent as usual, with an almost childish contrition. The debauch was mysteriously clouded. All he could remember was the fact of draining Nick's flask. This was clear. After that he had faint intimations of a hellish thirst—some effort to satisfy it. Through all his secret musings there ran a fear, a vague foreboding, but he could not define it. Memory would not work. He dwelt in a state of suspense, the victim of an intangible but real Nemesis. He expected something inimical to strike. Ned could see that something unusual was preying upon his father's mind and it troubled him deeply.

One thing that surprised Ned was the fact that his father had never referred to The Red Knight. He seemed to have utterly forgotten this darling of his life. Another week passed and the old man was about. Though correspondence was pouring in relative to the planting and culture of the new wheat, Edward Pullar evinced no interest in the matter. The heavy task of writing fell upon Ned. All efforts to rouse his father failed. He seemed unaware of the existence of the thing that had so lately made life new for him. At times an unspeakable fear swept over him as he realized how hopeless was this condition of disinterest.

Late one afternoon Ned was busy at his desk in diligent effort to reduce the piles of unanswered letters when a knock sounded upon the door. On opening, a strange face presented itself.

"Come in!" said Ned courteously.

"Is this Edward Pullar's ranch?" queried the man as he stepped in.

"It is," said Ned. "Have a chair."

The stranger seated himself and glanced about inquisitively.

"My name is Hank Foyle," said he. "I live up to Athabasca Landing. I was out on a hike in the timber limits when the letter got to me telling me about the deal. That is why I am a month late. I toted along last night and wrote my name into the papers this morning. Thought I'd take a squint at the farm and buildings before moseying back to the Landing. You've shore got a comfy joint here. Buildings first-rate."

Ned looked at his visitor with a puzzled face. Into the old man's eyes leaped a fear, vacillating and furtive, but real.

"I hardly understand," said Ned with an apologetic smile.

The other grinned.

"Naturally you don't know me," said the man, with a series of nods. "I am the guy that made the swap with you. Hank Foyle's my name—Foyle of Athabasca Landing."

The stranger paused, confident that the reiteration of his name would clear up matters. But Ned still looked at him with a nonplussed expression. His father's face had grown white while the nails of the old man's clenched hands dug into the flesh.

"Sorry I'm so dense," said Ned, with a good-natured laugh. "Would you mind going into detail a little?"

Foyle looked at him keenly, studying the firm mouth and chin and the direct eyes. There was something fearless in that face that hinted the possibility of a serious hitch.

"You ain't changed your mind?" said Foyle, with a narrowing of his eyelids. "You're a month late, farmer. The deal's salted away long ago, all regular signed and witnessed. You are no soft come-back, are you?"

Ned still smiled his perplexed smile.

"Very well!" said he affably. "What is the deal to which you refer? I'm open to rather detailed explanation, for I have heard of no such project."

The man rose and stepped up to Ned, looking curiously into his face.

"Say, Pard," said he quizzically, "are you Edward Pullar or just plain hired man?"

"There is Edward Pullar," said Ned, pointing to his father. "He is owner of this farm."

"You mean the man as was owner," corrected Foyle. "This half section belongs to me now."

As he spoke he looked at the old man.

"You're the Edward Pullar person what's scratched his name on them agreements?" was his observation as he studied the other contemplatively. "What's eating you now?"

Ned was surprised to see a look of terror dart from his father's eyes. There was a confusion about the manner of the old man that caused a little alarm in Ned himself.

"I—I don't understand," said Edward Pullar helplessly.

At his words an angry flush darkened Foyle's face.

"Like the hired man, here, you ain't wise to the deal, eh?" There was a note of derision in his voice. "Better put it straight," said he, with a shutting of his jaws. "You mean you don't want to understand. Getting foxy, old boy? It won't do, farmer. You can't string Hank Foyle. You'll have to tumble to facts. Hank Foyle shuts up like a clam; sticks like a leech. Noted for it. Your farm's mine and mine's yours, and you are due in Athabasca Landing agin the crops are in. That's what the paper says. You plant the crop here. I plant it at the Landing. Then we swaps farms and hikes for home. You'll have a whole section a scrub to wander through a-lookin' fur the cows."

"You are on the wrong farm," said the old man weakly. "We have not entered any such deal."

"You're Edward Pullar, what owned this place?" quizzed Foyle, with an impudent grin. "You haven't said so yet."

"I am Edward Pullar," was the acknowledgment.

"I reckon there ain't two Edward Pullars. Therefore I conclude there ain't any mistake either."

Deliberately Foyle drew a package from his pocket. Drawing out two papers he opened them carefully and, stooping, held them before the old man.

"Them's the real thing," said Foyle casually. "Take a

140

good, long squint. You'll find everything proper."

Edward Pullar examined the documents. They were, indeed, agreements of surrender and exchange signed by Foyle and a signature that was undoubtedly his own. The transaction was duly witnessed by Silas Marshall, magistrate. The old man stared at the papers, striving to catch the flying tags of mystery. Things seemed to clear a little, resulting, however, in deeper depression.

"I did not sign it," said he dazedly.

"Here, hired man," said Foyle, handing the papers to Ned. "Go right through 'em. You'll find them agreements square as an eight-inch bent."

Ned looked. A close study of the documents astonished him. The signature ascribed to his father was clearly his. As to Silas Marshall's there could be no mistake. He had seen it many a time. A seriousness spread over his face, mingling slowly with the amazement in it.

"This seems all right," said he, slowly perusing the papers. "But—but, of course, these papers are simply evidences of some fraud."

The date caught his eye. In a lightning play of thought he associated the mystery with the tragic trip to Pellawa. He straightened up and his chin rounded in a decisive firmness.

"Do you remember having anything to do with Cy Marshall, Dad?" was his quiet question.

"I do not," was the unhesitating reply. "And yet there is something familiar about it all, even those papers. I feel positive I have seen them before."

"Just possible!" commented Foyle insolently. "Probably caught a peep of 'em about the time you scrawled yer name."

"What agent put this through?" demanded Ned of Foyle.

"No kidding," was the fierce response. "You know all right. Sykes is the gent—Chesley Sykes—and a hum-dinger of an agent he is!"

Ned's eyes flamed upon the man.

"It is what I feared," said he, smiling the smile with which he faced McClure and his men in Sparrow's pool-room. "Here, take this rubbish, Mr. Foyle. You are either a crook or a dupe. Reddy Sykes has put through a real Sykes' deal. I want to warn you that it is the fraudulent plot of a clever swindler. This farm is my father's. I am Edward Pullar. There are two of us, and we are going to fight you. My father never signed away his homestead voluntarily. You can gain nothing by pressing the matter. For a stranger, you have been grossly insulting. Take my advice, tear up those papers and hit the trail for Athabasca Landing. You have about two minutes to pack up."

With a savage laugh Foyle folded the papers and deposited them carefully in his pocket.

"Pullar and Son," said he pugnaciously, "you're a pair of dang poor bluffers. But I'll call you. There ain't a flaw in the deal. This farm's mine. Come the time the grain's in you'll find Hank Foyle camping——"

He did not finish, for there was a swift motion on the part of Ned.

"Sorry, Hank!" said he with a grin. "But time's precious. Open the door, Dad."

With a wild laugh Foyle swung for the smiling face. Ned ducked and Foyle missed and continued the swing, the force of his empty blow spinning him around. When he had half completed the circle he felt himself seized by the scruff of the neck and the seat of his trousers and lifted high by the powerful derricks of Ned's arms. Through the door he was carried with arms windmilling and legs kicking, and dropped ignominiously into the cold receptacle of a melting drift. As he scrambled to his feet he heard the door shut. For a moment he hesitated, savaged with rage. But the memory of those steel arms was salutary, and he turned about and walked down the lane. For a mile or more there were mutterings filling the air about him such as would come fittingly from an Athabasca Lander on landing unexpectedly.

For a long time after Foyle's exit there was silence in the room. The two men were thinking hard. The last hour had been one of revelation to them both. Ned looked up about to speak, but desisted, hushed by the sight that met his eyes. His father sat huddled in a rocking-chair, his face buried in his hands. A pang pierced Ned as he realized the pitiable state of his father's mind.

Walking over, he laid his hand gently on the bowed head.

"Never mind, Dad," said he cheerily. "Reddy Sykes is not going to steal the homestead so easily. Of the foul work we are positive. We have only to track it down. We have until June to ferret out the rogues. You made a good fight, Dad. You were drugged. I have known that ever since I found you on the hill."

Raising his head he looked at Ned. Through the misery of grief there was a pathetic eagerness.

"Do—do you believe—I put up a fight, laddie?" was the trembling plea.

"I do, Dad," was the swift response. More Ned could not say, but he enveloped his father in a strong, steady embrace, tenderly holding the gray head that sobbed upon his breast. His eyes were wet. What they wanted just then was Kitty

Belaire.

XVIII

THE BIRD OF THE COULEE

There is life on the road—a rush into the April shine;
muffled clatter of galloping hoofs; the rhythmic sway of a
girlish form to the drum and flute of flying feet and
carolling lips. Youth and beauty in the saddle of spring!

Mary McClure was enjoying the leisure of the open trail
and halted Bobs on the floor of a coulee, a narrow, stream-
like depression with abrupt banks. It was a pretty green dip
zigzagging out of sight into east and west, and lined on
either bank with rounded clumps of willow. There were
gleams of a tiny creek. From the willows near her came the
soft twitter of nesting birds. Restraining the impatient Bobs,
she strove to discern the sweet singers. The cries were
familiar—all but one. It was a strange little call with a
plaintive, human-like wail and a ventriloquistic quality that
led one to think it came from far away. She was positive it
was the cry of some rare bird hidden in the leaves.

Swinging Bobs she trotted close to the trees. The birds,
alarmed, took flight down the coulee. She followed
cautiously and listened again, delighted at length to
distinguish the voice of the feathered stranger. A sudden
impulsive advance of Bobs, who essayed to crop a mouthful
of leaves, put the birds to flight once more. They doubled
back in a cloud of whirring wings. She was about to follow
when the cry of the strange bird came again out of the tree

144

before her. It alone had remained. She searched the tree, but no sign could she discover of the mysterious creature. Concluding at length that the sound came from a more distant clump, she rode further into the east. The sound now seemed much nearer. Tree after tree was passed, with the strangely recurring result of a growing clearness. She was deeply puzzled and intensely curious as to the enigma. Finally she reached the end of the bluff and still she could hear the call coming with an undoubted increase of volume. Pondering the circumstance she suddenly concluded that her bird was a weird illusion.

"Bobs!" she cried perplexedly, "our bird is not a bird. It is a disembodied voice."

Then as the cry broke clearly from a distance, she said in alarm:

"It is a human voice, Bobs. Somebody is in distress far down the coulee. Let us listen carefully. No champing of that bit, please."

The voice came again. It was indeed a human cry, smothered in some inexplicable way. The tone was one of plaintive terror. Urging the horse ahead, she cantered along the creek. Rounding a bend, she realized that the sound came from some point very near. Rising in her stirrups, she searched the coulee. The only unusual object that met her eye was the carcass of a horse. It lay in a sharp curve of the north bank close in. The noise was emanating from the vicinity of the dead animal. Riding toward it, she was thrilled to catch sight of a bit of red clothing.

"Bobs, Bobs! What a terrible thing!" was her horrified cry as she leaped to the ground beside the horse.

Crowded into a hole between the horse and the bank lay the figure of a little boy, scarcely five years of age. He was

145

stretched upon the ground with his small body half twisted into the bank. His bare limbs, right arm and left leg, were clutched in the steel fangs of a brace of great wolf traps. The dead horse had been used as a bait by some trapper who had set his traps between the horse and bank, at head and feet, in order to catch his wolf as it sought the entrails. Instead they had caught the curious child. Both limbs were torn and bloody from the grip of the biting steel as the boy twisted under the torture. His cry for help had been muffled by the encroaching bank.

The little fellow moaned for release as he caught sight of the girl. Looking up with wild, dazed eyes he cried:

"Take me, Mummie! Take me away!"

"You poor laddie!" comforted the girl. "I will help you, darling. You will be out in a minute. Do just what I say."

The sight of the small unfortunate made a powerful appeal to the sympathies. The little face was streaked with the pitiable wash of tears. The child could scarcely see. At a glance she saw that he was near collapse. She acted swiftly. Placing her foot upon the spring of the trap imprisoning the leg, she rested her whole weight upon it and it sank. With a quick motion of her deft fingers she opened the jaws and took out the limb. A moment later the arm, too, was free. Released, the little form rolled upon its back and lay helpless. Stooping she picked him up gently and carried him to the bank of the creek, laying him upon the grass.

"Lie here quiet, laddie," she enjoined in a soothing voice, "and I'll ride back to the village for a carriage. I'll be back in a few minutes."

But the child clung to her crying fearfully:

"Take me! Take me! Brubbie afraid!"

Kneeling beside him she gathered the small bundle into

146

her arms.

"I will not leave you, darling," she soothed, hushing his fears. "I will take you with me. Bobs will have to be a very gentle stretcher bearer. You must trust me, little one, and be careful to obey me. Bobs will carry us back. But first I must cover these poor torn limbs."

Producing clean bandages, with the resource of a former occasion, she wrapped the wounds securely from air and dirt. Then she placed the boy upon Bobs' neck while the intelligent brute stood motionless, obedient to her low voiced commands. Climbing carefully into the saddle she took the child in her arms and guiding Bobs by voice and knee, rode back along the coulee. The child slept almost instantly, lulled by the gentle pace of the horse and endearing cooings of the girl.

Aware that the surgeon's skill was urgently needed, she made her way to the doctor's office. He discovered her approach and running out to the curb relieved her of her burden. In a few words she informed him of her discovery of the boy and his misfortune.

"Will you come in?" said he. "You have done wonderfully and can help me with this operation. There is no nurse in the village just now."

"Gladly, if I can be of service," was the quick reply.

"Rest assured you can. With your assistance I shall be able to avoid the anæsthetic, though these wounds are a ragged mess. The poor little kid must have lain in those traps for hours. Pierre Leduc set them out for wolves. These curious little busybodies fall into surprising adventures. Brubbie will not forget this day for the rest of his life."

Swiftly the doctor performed his work, cleaning the frayed lacerations and stitching with nimble address, while

Mary beguiled the boy from his pain by the charm of her caress and the soothing touch of her woman's hand.

"There now, Brubbie!" said the doctor at length. "You are fit. Come, we'll take you to your mother. Miss McClure had better come along and take charge of this most difficult phase of the operation. Will you, Miss McClure?"

"Still at your service, Doctor. But who is Brubbie, as you call him?"

"Brubbie? Why, Brubbie is the young scamp of Pellawa, general town favourite and Nick Ford's baby. Brubbie is an incorrigible little vagrant. I'll warrant his mother hasn't even missed him. This will be some shock to her."

It was a very startled and white-faced woman who gathered the small form to her breast.

"Mummie, Mummie!" was the penitent cry. "Brubbie run away. He step on traps and dey bite him. Brubbie think he will die and cry, cry, cry. But the leddy come and take Brubbie out of the traps and bring him home on the nice horse. Oo, oo!"

He encircled the woman's neck with a strangling hug.

Mary smiled, relieved that the explanation had been made.

"Brubbie has given you all the facts, Mrs. Ford," corroborated she. "I heard the cry of a strange bird in the coulee and followed it. The bird turned out to be Brubbie. Bobs carried him to the doctor here, who has fixed him up splendidly. He will soon be around again."

The mother was dumb. For some minutes she could only nestle the child to her breast. Suddenly, as she thought upon the circumstance, a shudder swept her. A gruesome possibility had occurred to her.

"What would have happened to my baby if you had not

heard him crying, Miss McClure? To-night the wolves would have come. God bless you for this."

The woman's eyes filled with tears. Under the impulse of her natural gratitude she seized the girl's hand and kissed it reverently.

"You saved Brubbie! You saved him! You saved him!" she cried again and again, in a quiet, grateful voice. "Nick will thank you with all his heart. Cod bless you!"

As Mary passed through the coulee on her way home, she pulled Bobs again and listened to the birds afresh. This time the strange call was missing and a serious look crept into the girl's eyes as she thought upon it.

"Little birds!" she whispered. "Happy little birds! Your sweet singing saved a dear little life to-day."

The happiest musings attended her as she let Bobs follow the trail of his own sweet will. The mission of the birds was not yet ended.

XIX

CHESLEY SYKES UNCOVERS HIS HAND

The night of the day upon which Mary McClure hunted the bird of the coulee, an interesting council was held in the realty office of Reddy Sykes. The councillors comprised McClure, Foyle and the agent himself. They sat about the flat-topped desk, three shadows in the blue fog of the dim lamplight. There were the usual convivial evidences, Foyle having been the first to arrive at that affable condition obtaining in the mazy borderlands of sobriety and inebriety.

"Pards!" said he, smashing the desk with his open hand, "I'm taking yer lead and tickled to do it. Yer shore handing me the whole deck. I'll see that Ford gets his little share all right and a bit over."

"You've tumbled, Foyle," replied Sykes. "You have been mighty apt at getting the hang of things. You have nothing to do but sit tight. I give my cheerful and professional guarantee there isn't a flaw in the deal. If Pullar is fool enough to hold you off we'll turn on the screw and evict him. The law is the prettiest, most efficient automatic instrument invented by the genius of that good fellow, man. The law is behind us everywhere. Don't you do any talking. Meanwhile, mosey around and make yourself generally useful. That bunch of scrub out of Athabasca Landing won't need your tender offices any more. Leave it to Pullar and Son. They are mighty good farmers."

"Ha! That's the big noise!" agreed Foyle, with a chuckle. "I've taken to the climate hereabouts. Got to stay. Doctor's orders. Ha, ha! You'll find Hank Foyle sticking around any old time you want him."

"You're a good sort," commended Sykes warmly. "I'll want the help of a reliable man in a day or two. In fact I'll want you bad, Hank."

"Put it here," cried Foyle, springing to his feet with extended hand. "I'm spoiling for exercise. Used to scrubbing, you know. Anything you want done kind of quiet-like just drop a wink."

"Hank, you're a game sport," was the hearty response. Then he added: "You're a marked man. I'll trail you when I want you. And now, this ends our confab for the present. Rob and I have a pile of work to go through before we get out of here to-night. You are overdue at the Dominion

House. Bye, bye!"

Foyle laughed good-naturedly.

"I'll scoot," said he. "And don't forget I'm handy when you want a leg up."

For a considerable time after he left there was silence between the partners. Then McClure fixed his eyes curiously on Sykes. There was something in his companion's eyes he had never seen there before. He instantly realized that something momentous was being debated in the mind of the agent.

"Pulling a bluff on Hank just now?" was his quizz.

"Better have an eye-opener, Rob," was the reply, as he pushed a glass and bottle to his companion's elbow. "You are keen enough on some things and mighty dense on others. I have a surprise for you. In a few days I am pulling down my shingle."

McClure knit his eyebrows in perplexity.

"This is one thing you've been hopelessly opaque on, Rob," said he as he casually filled his own glass. "Did you expect I had come to stay?"

"No-o," was the slow reply. "I knew you had a card up your sleeve. I hold no hand in the game."

Sykes smiled.

"A clear case of cobwebs," observed the other to himself. "You are in this game very much and have been all along. There will be nothing obscure in your mind as to my intentions when I'm through with you to-night. Since the onus of revelation is upon me you will maintain a purely receptive attitude. This is coming to me.

"Now to begin. Here are some photographs. You have heard of John Sykes, millionaire broker? Here he is and there is the mater. This is our hang-out on the Crescent.

151

John Sykes is a rather close relative of mine. Here is the prospectus of Sykes and Sykes, the new partnership replacing John Sykes. I hold a third of the stock, the old man the balance."

Sykes paused while the other was examining the photographs. McClure was visibly impressed. The faces looking at him were handsomely autocratic. John Sykes had a set to his jaw that was familiar.

"They have some class," said he, handing back the photographs. "This looks like the firm may have a pretty tidy turnover."

He continued to make a careful perusal of the prospectus.

"Cold figures," agreed Sykes. "We have the best connections, private wires through to London, New York, etc., all of which means a big place in the financial world. Here are our ratings."

McClure looked them over, his eyes evincing the most intense interest. Before he could speak Sykes thrust into his hand a paper.

"A little bit of Who's Who? Read it over; it will acquaint you with public opinion. It speaks well of us."

As McClure finished he looked up, his eye fascinated by some alluring mental object. Sykes was sitting back nonchalantly in his swivel chair, his partially emptied glass poised in his hand. He observed his companion with a smile.

"What do you make of it all?" was his question.

"It is a great surprise to me and yet—I long ago surmised something like this. I knew of John Sykes as a prominent financier, but had not the faintest idea there was any connection between you."

"There may not be," said Sykes, with a peculiar laugh. "I may be faking. It would be easy to frame up a setting like this."

McClure shook his head.

"You look too much like John Sykes. He is the only man I have ever seen with a jaw like yours."

Sykes laughed silently at the personal allusion as he handed over another photograph.

"Here," said he, "is a picture the mater insisted on having."

It was a likeness of himself and his mother.

"I'll complete this personal art exhibition by troubling you to run through this folio."

It was a set of athletic photographs, splendid pictures of an eight-oared crew. In the first a superb figure stood before him holding a long scull. In the second the athlete was seated in a single shell, his sculls poised for the long sweep. There were others of the "Eight" in various poses of rest and action, several with the setting of foreign regattas. One caught the crew sweeping along the Thames. The athlete was Sykes.

"McClure!" said he seriously, "I had a fairly free fling in the younger days. But I kept the going under hand. Do you think the type of physical man you see there would go very far wrong?"

McClure laughed in some embarrassment.

"No use putting such a decision up to me," said he. "But you shape up prime in your racing stumps."

"That will do," commented Sykes with a grin. "The art display is over. You may think this irrelevant to the business in hand. Perhaps it is. At any rate keep everything you have learned in the back of your head while I spiel a bit.

"You are right in your guess. I am not in Pellawa to push petty finance. I am here hunting the biggest game that runs. We have been associated in some rustic ventures and they have not all come through. Forget it. These have been trivial undertakings. Study that Who's Who? and you'll find that I get every big thing I go after. I am after the biggest thing right now I have ever set out to lift. You probably can tell me what it is."

McClure shook his head.

"I am not guessing to-night," said he, holding Sykes' glance.

"Then prepare for a sweeping away of all cobwebs. My sole object in this visit to Pellawa, Rob, is your daughter, Miss Mary McClure. I have been playing the game for that stake right through. The time has come for a show-down. It is up to us to deal a new hand. I have approached your girl from every conceivable angle. She is obdurate. There is a mighty good reason. She is the victim of a silly infatuation. She has a local rube."

McClure sprang to his feet.

"It's a lie!" was the swift retort.

Sykes smiled darkly, shaking his head.

"No, Rob, this is not hearsay. This is personal knowledge. I hold the facts and I will lay them before you — later. There is this infatuation. These youthful attachments seldom result in happy matrimonial alliances. This amour is no more promising than any other. It is not disturbing and need have no undesirable results if we act quickly. I am willing to accept Mary on any terms and by means of any expedient. I offer her everything a woman could desire. Give me your complete coöperation in my plan to gain my purpose and I promise you unheard-of compensation. Just a

154

moment!"

He lifted his hand silencing McClure, who was about to speak.

"I have told you to listen while I spiel. That is the only thing for you to do yet. I want you to be confident of this. With Mary as my wife, she will gain everything and lose nothing. For yourself it means a chance that does not come to one man in a million.

"I have watched you, Rob McClure, as you went to it in this world of small farmers. You are too big a man for Pellawa. Don't misunderstand me. I do not propose to flatter you. What I am about to propose is frankly my own project to gain my personal purposes. Were it not for this I certainly would not dream of handing out the deal I am going to offer you. But the fact remains. You have the gray matter to come through if you decide to avail yourself of this opportunity. You will be at home in the big financial world. Take a look at that rating."

He handed his companion a certified document.

"A third of that is mine. That gets me into seven figures. What is your own rating, land and all?"

McClure calculated swiftly.

"Roughly, seventy-five thousand."

"Rather a difference! However, it is not your fault. It is your fate. You have done wonderfully well. But you have been playing a small game. I had the luck to be reared in a bigger world. The pater assures me that I have added a million to the total during my university years when I had been supposedly engaged in the serious task of reading law. You may think this egotism or even bluff. Perhaps it is."

McClure read the fellow's face. He was instantly convinced of the truth of his words. He was silent.

"Now, Rob!" said Sykes, levelling at the other a glance at once piercing and calculating. "Take in what I am about to say. It means tremendous things for you. At the same time what may seem remarkable to you is as nothing to me compared with the big thing I am out after. Help me to get this thing and—— But wait a minute. My rating upsets yours thirty to one. How would a ratio of fifty-fifty place you? Think in the totals. A million and a quarter! You will never reach that in this little world of Pellawa. Never. Yet that would be commensurate with your sheer ability. Are you ready to take in that dream? Listen, Rob McClure! It is yours now, to-day. I have an immense mellon. I will cut that mellon exactly in half and give you one half for the hand of Mary McClure. I offer you a partnership on the basis of fifty-fifty. To show that I mean business, I will give half the legal grip even before Mary becomes my wife. The balance after. There shall be this one stipulation only. The partnership is conditioned on the fact that Mary joins hands with me in a legal marriage."

Sykes ceased to talk.

McClure was mute, the great eyes darting flames. Sykes knew that the crucial moment had arrived. For months he had fostered this friendship, spun his web. Would the victim break through the mesh and go free? The farmer looked at him, his face convulsed in conflict. At one instant the eagerness of an overmastering ambition looked out craftily; the next it was swept with a mighty anger. While the fierce debate raged, Sykes addressed him in a low, steadying voice.

"Rob," said he considerately, "this is a fairly sizable proposition. Don't make a snap decision and regret— anything. Keep the lid on a little longer. You have not yet heard all. You have not learned who is the rube that has fascinated Mary. Perhaps you already know or can guess?"

"I will not guess," he flung out fiercely. "There is nothing in it. If there had been, Mary would have let me know long ago. She has never hinted such an attachment."

"You are logical, Rob. But you are wrong. You have hit the wrong premise. Sometimes a good girl is induced into a clandestine amour. It has often happened. It has happened now. Unsympathetic parents are not auspicious persons in which to confide the tender sentiments. The parent might have a positive hostility to the dear object of one's regard. This is pointedly true in your own case. I know there is no love lost between you. And now you know the party."

McClure leaned forward, a sudden intelligence flashing a wild light in his eye.

"You don't mean — —?"

McClure read Sykes' cold, bright eyes. He understood.

"It is Ned Pullar?"

"Pullar's the man, Ned Pullar," was the deliberate agreement.

Slowly the indecision vanished from McClure's face and in its place appeared a black resolution. A malignant light darted from his eyes. Seizing the neck of the black bottle before him, he clutched it menacingly, as if about to hurl it at his companion.

"Rather be excused," said Sykes, lifting a defensive hand. "Remember I am not Pullar."

Banging the bottle on the desk, McClure whirled about and began pacing about the room, muttering vengeful execration, oblivious apparently of the other's presence.

At this moment of his fell triumph, the real Sykes looked forth once more. A repulsive delight played in his eyes and they shut to, in a sort of gloating muse. While the

157

evil light glittered through the lashes, an unsightly grin contorted his face, drawing slowly to a wolfish snarl about mouth and nose. The face was grotesque and hideous to look upon. Could he have trained one rational, though fleeting glance upon that unspeakable face, McClure would surely have been forewarned. But he was blind with rage. Out of the fury of that fatal moment flew the foul bird of a pitiless resolution. He chuckled balefully. At the sound Sykes laughed softly. Ripping out an oath McClure whirled about. Thrusting his head forward he searched Sykes' face with blazing eyes. He was too slow, however. The malign thing had hidden itself with swift adroitness. What he saw was the open, sympathetic countenance of a gentleman.

"I want the facts," challenged McClure. "What do you know?"

Dissembling his intensity of interest, Sykes divulged what information he deemed expedient to his purpose. The effect on McClure was powerfully cumulative.

"Look here," said the agent finally, picking up a photograph of the eight-oared crew. "You did not detect this party."

McClure looked surprised to recognize the face of Ned Pullar.

"Our coach selected Pullar for number seven to hold my oar," explained Sykes. "Until Pullar caught the place we had trouble holding balance. With his arrival the kink smoothed out magically and we went overseas a wonder crew. He held my stroke. Pullar is the only man who ever did. You have not yet realized what this man Pullar is capable of. He takes the inside every time and sets a killing pace. He'll beat you out now like he faded you in the threshing game unless you take my way to kill him. I'll come across with the specific code any time you want it. You must act swiftly and stick it. The stake is big. For me, it means one thing only—Mary McClure. For Mary, it means a brilliant chance. For you it means a flying start in the big world where big men hold the throttle. For both you and me it means the smashing of Pullar."

He paused. The two men eyed each other, McClure with flaming, searching glance, Sykes with steady, persistent gaze and eyes that poured upon the other the mesmeric power of will.

"I have had my say," said Sykes quietly, holding that compelling glance. "I have been straight. It is up to you."

For a long time there was silence in the room. Then McClure spoke slowly, weighing each word, held from a full committal by some sudden instinct of caution.

"I believe you, Sykes," was his low-voiced admission. "At present I don't see anything against your plan. But it is a big thing, and you have rushed it up to me. I want time to think. I'll not say just now whether I'll hook up with your offer or not. I have a stipulation to hand you before we go ahead. You must see the chit yourself and make her a fair proposition. Put it straight to her and make it as rosy as you can. If she throws you down I'll probably take a hand."

Sykes nodded his head in reluctant acquiescence.

"Very well," said he. "I'll meet you. I'll talk to the little girl, though I know it will do no good. It may stampede her into some decision that will queer our game. She is no fool."

"I insist," said McClure firmly. "Get busy. In the meantime I'll catch my feet. For to-night I have had enough."

Seizing his hat, McClure took his abrupt departure.

As he shut the door Sykes put out the lamp. Taking a

cigarette from his pocket he struck a match and proceeded to light it. In the red glow his face seemed to float out of the black pall of the night, an impish thing from the pit. The grin of the wolf snarled off the lips as they opened to emit a soft, chuckling laugh.

XX

A FAWN AT BAY

The following afternoon Mary McClure sat pensively at her piano, her spirit awander in the dulcet shadowlands of an improviso. She was pondering a remarkable thing. At that moment her parents were out for a jaunt in the Valley, the first in years. She recalled the pleasure lighting her mother's face as she accepted the unique proposal. Hope of happier relations had stirred in her breast. For all the bright little circumstance there was a query in Mary's mind that drew minor strains from the plaintive piano.

It was some weeks since she had seen Ned Pullar. They had then agreed to terminate their covert meetings, hoping for a turn in the wheel of fate that would be auspicious. She was deeply troubled over rumours that hinted embarrassment for Ned and his father. She had not learned the true facts but had drawn shrewd deductions from the reports of Mrs. Grundy. Lately a fear had obsessed her. She tried to banish the thought in view of the glad incident of the afternoon, but those minor vagaries would persist in stealing from her fingers.

A chat with Margaret Grant had informed her of the presence of the stranger Foyle as inimical to Ned. The old homestead was in some way involved. Shortly after her chat with Margaret she had observed her father in friendly conversation with Foyle before the office of Chesley Sykes. At the sight a shadow had flitted through her mind. Was her father involved in Ned's trouble?

She had abandoned herself to a sombre brooding upon this disquieting theme when a knock sounded upon the door. It startled her, for she was alone. Lifting her hands from the keys, she went to the door. On opening she was confronted with the great figure of Chesley Sykes. A smile lit his handsome face. Touching his hat with graceful courtesy, he greeted her respectfully.

"Good-day, Miss McClure!" was his quiet salute.

At the sound of his voice the episode at the door flashed into her mind. She regretted the absence of her parents.

Hospitality forbade rudeness and she invited him within.

"I have come to see you, yourself," said he, smiling at her formality. "I am heartily glad there is nobody else about. I have been anxious to crave your pardon for my part in the incident at the door. It was inexcusable and foolish, I acknowledge. I am sorry."

The girl looked away with serious face. Instinct warned her against the man, but his tone and manner were agreeably penitent. She believed him.

"I do not hold grudges, Mr. Sykes," was her reply. "I remember the matter well and I am glad to forget it, since you desire it."

"That relieves me," was the pleased reply. "I promise to observe the good old conventions in the future. There was something extenuating, had you known it. Have you no suspicion of what a real fact lay behind that silly act? Of that fact I am not ashamed."

Mary offered no surmise and moved to the window, where she became absorbed in the world without.

"I want to talk some things over to-day," said he frankly,

162

moving to her side. "This is probably the last time I shall solicit your forbearance. I am leaving Pellawa.

"You know of the college years and the unswerving interest a certain student at law took in a certain small co-ed. That interest had deepened during these days in Pellawa. You and you alone, Mary McClure, are the reason for my presence here. I have been chasing the gleam. I have been bitterly disappointed. The rustic life has not drawn us any nearer. And yet—I—I have not thrown up the sponge. I am not resigning you, Mary. That is my purpose here to-day. I want to let you know this. I have only one objective, only one dream in the alluring puzzle called life, and that is, Mary McClure. My single ambition is to win you for my wife. Some day, Mary, will you marry me?"

The girl turned toward him, astounded at his impudence, a flush rising in her cheeks. At sight of him she could not doubt his sincerity.

"Mr. Sykes," she said quickly, "you have no right to make such an approach to me."

"Only the right of a mighty big regard that keeps on growing without any especial attention from the most desirable quarter."

She remained silent a moment, suddenly reflective.

"Perhaps you are right," she said thoughtfully. "If you are, you already know my answer. I can never become the wife of Chesley Sykes. Never."

Her manner was so emphatic, so deliberate, that the confidence of the man received a jolt. He heard the ring of steel on steel and looked in wonder at the dainty antagonist.

"I am sure you will not approach me again," said she in a manner he realized was imperative. Then she smiled. "You are Daddy's friend," said she, with a pleasant courtesy. "I

163

will not forget that."

There followed a long silence. At length she looked up. His face was a surprise to her. There was no vexation, no displeasure. Instead, the passion of the man expressed itself in a great friendliness. There was something else that disturbed her. It was a confidence, an assurance, a determination not to be denied.

With a shrug of his shoulders he seemed to throw off the gloom that attended his defeat and, smiling ingenuously, said:

"Play for me that sweet thing you were dreaming over when I broke up your paradise."

She shook her head.

"No," was her quiet refusal. "I cannot. My mood is not musical any longer. I hear Father's bells. He will be better able to entertain you."

"Sorry you cannot draw to me to-day," said he regretfully, taking up his hat. "But your mood will change. Some day you will take a delight in delighting me. I, myself, am not now in a frame of mind to be companionable. It is better that I return to Pellawa. Give my regards to your parents. And remember," enjoined he with peculiar emphasis, "remember that I am still on the trail of my distracting little Will-o'-the-wisp."

Sykes had gone but a few minutes when Helen McClure entered. Her face was flushed and unhappy. Gathering Mary into her arms, she kissed her with impulsive tenderness.

"Whatever happens, darling," she whispered hurriedly, "follow your heart. The happiness of us all depends upon it, though it may seem otherwise."

"Mother!" said the girl, excitement welling up in her eyes. "How troubled you are! What is it?"

"I am a little anxious for you," said the mother, disengaging herself gently from Mary's clasp. "Your father has been talking to me of your prospects. He wishes to see you in the office. He is coming now. If you follow your heart all will some day be well."

With the words she bestowed upon Mary a clinging caress.

The girl walked hesitantly to the office and stood looking out of the window as she awaited her father. She was threatened with panic but grew composed as she heard his footsteps in the hall. She turned as he entered and lifted her head, meeting his great eyes with the clear gaze of her own. He, too, was steeling himself to the interview. His unsmiling face distressed her. Passing by her, he seated himself in his office chair and whirled about. Before he could look up to where she stood he was surprised to feel the touch of her hands upon his head. Enfolding him in her arms, she kissed his brow. A thrill swept over him. For an instant he looked with the inner eye upon his own soul. He knew it to be unnatural, brutal.

"Daddy!" she whispered. "Let me tell you all before you speak."

Gently, but with a steady, rigid motion of his hands, he pressed her back. The tenderness that had betrayed him for but an instant vanished.

"We'll see about that in a moment," was the cold reply. "I want to ask you a few questions before you tell your story. Sykes tells me he had a talk with you this afternoon."

"A diplomatic conversation," corrected Mary, with a faint smile.

"What did he say?"

"A great deal. It was not, after all, very much of a

conversation. It was a declaration. I almost fancied he was issuing a veiled ultimatum. He did, however, ask me a pointed question and I gave him a blunt reply."

"You refused him?"

"Yes."

"Do you know Sykes?"

"Too wisely and too well. His father is a wealthy broker; his mother a delightful aristocrat and a very fashionable lady. They live in a dreamland on The Crescent shut in with exclusive hedges amid the bloom of wonderful flowers. Their well-trimmed terraces run down to the water's edge. Sykes is a fellow-student of some years' duration. He has seemed to take rather more than a mild interest in the lone hope of the McClures. But I do not like him, Dad. I like Ned."

"So they tell me."

"I love Ned, Dad," was the gentle confession.

"But Sykes is a gentleman," said McClure testily.

"Ned is a man. I love a man, a real man, Dad."

McClure rose to his feet, the old passion rising afresh.

"I cannot agree with you. A man would not sneak into the bluffs to be alone with the girl he respects."

The stroke drew blood. A flush swept over the sensitive face.

"I did meet Ned once alone by accident," was the admission. "At all other times Margaret Grant joined us. We have not had even these interviews for weeks."

"How long have you been encouraging Pullar?"

"Ned and I became intimate in our first year at the University."

"Why did you not tell me?"

The girl looked pleadingly into the eyes that grew each

166

moment more chill. She halted in her reply, irresolute and deeply troubled. Had she the courage to drag the family skeleton into the light? She dropped her eyes and pondered. When she lifted them they were wet with tears.

"Come!" was the brusque command. "Tell me why you and Pullar skulk about the ravines like a pair of coyotes."

"The reason I have not confided in you, Father," said the girl slowly, "is because of your strange enmity for Ned. That, however, would not have been a sufficient reason had it not been for the cruel thing that has robbed Mother and me of our husband and Daddy. You have become a stranger to us. We do not tell these dear tales to—strangers. I could love you, Father, if you did not trample our hearts with your cruel heels."

At her words McClure shrank back. He scarcely believed his ears. Yet it was little Mary who stood before him self-possessed and unafraid, smiting his conscience with her gentle voice. Her eyes were imploring and beautiful, with a yearning he could not face. With an impatient shrug he turned away.

"What would we have gained," continued the girl, "had I told you of my intimacy with the man you hate? It would have resulted in only deeper misery for our home. It is cruel of me to talk like this, but it is the truth. Mother suffers continuous anguish, hiding it from us as only her wonderful love can devise. This is my only reason for loving Ned in secret. We are not afraid to let the world know of it. It already knows. As you well know, Ned fears nothing, not even the anger of Rob McClure."

The sight of the girl with her earnest eyes and tremulous lips touched the buried ruth of the man. At her frank arraignment he felt the stirrings of a compunction

167

that was new. Her piteous helplessness held off from him by his own chill unrelenting pierced him to a depth she little dreamed. The memory of her suppliant figure haunted him through the after years.

But he resisted. A sudden bracing of the unyielding will stiffened his wavering resolution. As is usual when a man stifles the inner voice, Rob McClure swung instantly to the opposite extreme. "Here," he mused, "is this daughter of mine, browbeating me rather than giving me dutiful obedience." He was about to lash her with scandalous insinuation when the ulterior object recurred to him. He forthwith tempered his rage with a wise craftiness.

"You have given a strange reason," said he judicially. "I will not give my consent to your friendship with such a hound. Why not consider a red-blooded man like Chesley Sykes? He is intelligent, educated, wealthy and delightfully congenial. In addition, he is your father's close friend. Never before have I used my authority. But now I forbid you to have anything to do with Pullar. Turn your attention to something that offers you a future."

"You mean that I must break my engagement with Ned?"

"I do," was the adamant response.

At the brutal tone a swift change came over the girl. While an infinite suffering looked out of her eyes she stood erect and proud.

"Do you also command that I shall accept Chesley Sykes in Ned's place?"

Her voice had the ring that had shaken the confidence of Sykes but a short time before. He felt the danger in it and tempered his reply.

"No, Mary! I don't command. I urge you."

"But you have as much right to command me to marry Chesley Sykes as you have to forbid my friendship with Ned Pullar. Why not, then?"

McClure paused a moment, calculating her intention.

"I have the right to do either," was the triumphant reply. There was a threat in his voice.

The girl looked at him a moment, her face aquiver with pain. The anguish of her emotion blanched cheeks and lips. She addressed him in a voice strange for its quality of renunciation.

"Father," said she, "your words are terrible to me. They mean that you would deprive me of your affection—of my home. You have not the right to command me to do a wrong. That is not the prerogative of even a parent. As for Chesley Sykes, I abhor him as unscrupulous and cruel. The more I know of him the less I can discover to admire. I will never marry him. On the other hand, some day I shall marry Ned. You misunderstand him. He is not your enemy. He would be a real friend. I shall be forced to disobey you, Father."

Reluctantly the girl turned away and walked to the door.

McClure was the victim of an overwhelming rage. Never had he been so stoutly withstood. It galled him to know that his daughter was right. In logic of brain and ethics she had worsted him. He was eager for savage retort, but the offer of Sykes dangled before him like golden fruit. The venom of his rage would destroy it. So he was cunning and remained silent.

"Just a moment, Mary," said he in a conciliatory voice.

She turned eagerly toward him.

"I would not force you to do anything you do not wish

to do," said he. "But do not be rash. Think it all over carefully. Your home is here. It will always be so. Perhaps after a time you will be able to meet my wishes."

Bitterly disappointed, the girl turned away. She was also surprised. Her father, though beyond doubt in a violent rage, had acquiesced to her will. Amid all the turmoil of her distress she recalled the nonchalance of Chesley Sykes as she refused his proposal. As with him, her father seemed not so greatly disappointed. As she pondered the enigma a thought flitted into her mind that caused a cold chill to clutch at her heart.

Without a reply she passed through the door.

XXI
THE COUNTERPLOT

Following their interview with Mary, Rob McClure and Sykes concluded it expedient to make a flying visit to the city. Mary found her father in remarkably good humour on his return. So affable was his mood that she was beginning to hope for a reprieve of the fates to avert the calamity she feared. But her hope was short lived. Riding into the stable after a long evening canter through the Valley she was greeted pleasantly by her father.

"Is Bobs going good to-day?" was his interested question.

"Bobs never misses," was the reply. "He danced along in wonderful form, but I could not enter into his gaiety. I bounced around upon his back a most unresponsive dreamer."

He lifted his eyebrows.

"Surely you are not yet worrying over our conversation?"

The kindliness of his tone drew the simple admission:

"Yes, Daddy."

"Have you decided to fall in with your good prospects?"

She studied his eyes with a keenness that alarmed him. He read her answer in the wearied face and, speaking quickly, forestalled her reply.

"I will say no more about Ned Pullar," said he. "I am willing to leave it all with you. I am confident you will see after a while that it is best to forget him. Lest you should act rashly I want you to know that not only your own happiness but my future career rests wholly with you. I am now a partner in the new firm of brokers, Sykes, McClure and Sykes. Nothing but a foolish spurning of your wonderful opportunity with Chesley Sykes can hold back the most astonishing possibilities for us all."

The girl's head drooped. She realized that snares were being skilfully and cruelly laid. To her father she had become a mere chattel.

"Daddy," she said gently, "it grieves me to disobey you, to disappoint you. But once for all you must know that no inducement, however tempting to me or however disappointing to you in my refusal of it, will persuade me to do the thing you urge."

Again to her surprise, he showed no great chagrin. Instead he betrayed an over anxiety in his desire to conciliate her.

Through the long, sleepless hours of the night she brooded, striving to think a way out. The sense of personal peril grew upon her. She remembered the light in her father's eyes as he told her of his good fortune. She shuddered as she recalled it. In the morning, as she rode over the Valley, she decided to see Ned at the earliest moment.

Rob McClure was greatly alarmed at the invulnerable front the girl presented. Arrived in his office, he drew a bundle of documents from a drawer and examined them. The title fascinated him. He rocked back in his chair to con its lure when his eyes caught the vision of the two faces above. Suddenly he realized that upon the inscrutable and inviolable will behind the sweet face of Mary rested his fortune. With Mary and not with himself rested the decision that should ratify or destroy his arrangement with Sykes. It all depended upon the girl above with the innocent face. Could he leave it to her? A keen study of the pure eye and firm brow shook his confidence in a desirable outcome. Rising, he leaned toward the picture with an abandon that betrayed his intensity of desire.

"Mary!" he whispered. "You will throw me down. I feel it. Sykes is right. There is no other way. The little chit is blind. I shall be forced to do it. I will see Sykes. She will surrender when there is nothing else to do."

This colloquy with the silent photograph had momentous results for the fair original.

At noon there was the clatter of hoofs outside the Pullar homestead and the winding of a silvery halloo. Ned went out.

"To saddle!" cried Mary as Ned appeared. "Get Darkey and come! We'll ride at high noon! We'll brew a tale on the King's Highway."

Aware that some serious matter prompted Mary's visit

Ned was up on Darkey in a trice and they rode out on an endless trail of the undulating plain. When deep out in the lonely stretch Mary drew Bobs to a walk.

"Ned," she said, "are you prepared for a most unusual proposition?"

"Anything you propose will meet with my entire support."

"Then hear me. The danger you feared so long ago is imminent. Father has learned of our engagement from the lips of Chesley Sykes. I have talked with Father. You can easily surmise what that interview involved. But a few minutes before Sykes had submitted a personal offer to the present rider of Bobs. The offer was declined respectfully if summarily. Father has backed his friend and forbids me you, Ned. I am to instantly and casually forget you. In the selfsame instant I am to foster the tenderest regard for Sykes. This very interview is a disobedience."

She paused, looking up at Ned, her face a compound of anxiety and mischief. Ned sent Darkey to Bobs' flank and threw his arm about the lithe little rider.

"Mary," said he, "you are a brave girl. Will you marry me to-day? This very day?"

"Hush, Ned!" was her cry as she placed her hand upon his lips. "You are stealing my fire. That is my proposition. Only I put it this way. Will you marry me not to-day or to-morrow but the day after?"

"I'll marry you to-day and to-morrow and the day after," was the happy response. "But why put it off?"

"Now I have broken the ice, Ned, it will be easier. I am a frightened little prairie chicken running for cover. I was going to ask you to do this trifling thing for me the day after to-morrow when you anticipated by two days. It is

173

very good of my big farmer to ask no questions and to be willing even to advance dates, but I have a little to say in justification of this bold visit.

"Since my interview with Father the firm of Sykes and Sykes has become the firm of Sykes, McClure and Sykes. Last night Father informed me that if I throw down Chesley Sykes I therewith crash to the ground his whole brilliant future—that is Father's."

"You are in a hard place, Mary," said Ned solicitously. "It is troubling you terribly despite your brave front. You are grieving, I know."

"A little worried, Ned," was the simple acknowledgment. "It has been difficult and it will be. It is not Father's anger that has driven me to you. It is abject fear. I am afraid of Sykes—and Father. I turn down Sykes. It does not anger him. He remains congenial. I withstand Father and promise to wreck his whole career. He is scarcely disturbed. Why are they not provoked? Because they are not. They are confident of realizing the thing they want. Ned, I have become such a frightened little goose that I carry this."

She drew an automatic gun from some mysterious repository in the breast of her riding habit. At sight of the weapon Ned's eyes flashed their dangerous light.

"You are wise to provide defense," said he soberly, "since your enemy is Sykes. Your intuition has not led you astray. For all his suavity and culture Sykes is a savage. He is the monster our civilization rears in the lap of luxury. He has been trained to expect full satiation of his desires. He has a maxim that he gets what he goes after. He knows utterly nothing of self-mastery. He has never denied himself. He never will. Nor will he yield to fate. You are in great danger and have been for months. Some conspiracy is on foot. Its

174

execution may be a matter of but a few hours. There is but one thing to do, Mary. You must marry me to-day."

The girl looked into his eyes.

"I am glad you understand," said she. "I will marry you, Ned, but at the time I have proposed. They shall lead me into nothing undesirable before then. To-day, to-night I want to myself to think it all out. To-morrow I shall teach and to-morrow night I shall tell all to Mother and consult with her. She will agree to our marriage upon 'the day after.'"

Ned demurred but to no purpose.

"Since you insist on your date," said Ned with a smile, "will you grant me the privilege of planning the elopement?"

"Your plans first. This is my escapade."

"Very well. The 'day after' you ride out to The Craggs as usual. I shall meet you at the Peak of the Buffalo Trails and together we shall ride to The Fort. It is only a canter of twenty miles. There we shall be wed in the parsonage of Oliver Darwin. He is our good friend. Father will go over to the school and inform the children that Miss McClure is 'indisposed.'"

"My saddle for a bridal coach! Ned! That is an inspiration. We'll ride the winding trail into the mystic West."

She held her lips to him and their kiss was the pure caress of a noble passion.

That night Ned rode to The Fort and made full arrangements, reaching home by the gray light of dawn.

XXII

WOLVES

The pastime of draw poker was engaging the energies of Sykes, McClure, Foyle, Snoopy Bill and their gang of familiars. The hour ran long past the closing time of eleven P.M.

Though stakes had flown high the game had failed to catch the interest of Rob McClure. He played his hand with a detachment that threw him open to heavy losses. So far he had escaped. His mind was the battle ground of a struggle he had not calculated on. Sykes watched him covertly all evening, striving to pierce the mask of his unsmiling face. It delighted him to trace the ruthless lines about the mouth. On the other hand it perturbed him not a little to see distinct evidences of indecision. With the deliberate purpose of fostering the reckless mood Sykes kept up a perpetual toasting. He toasted the pot, the queens and the aces all in turn, drinking lightly himself while McClure took copious draughts. With all his apathy McClure won regularly while Sykes lost as steadily. The double-plying of the farmer with the frequently recurring toast and an unswerving success in the game was fast realizing Sykes' purpose. He was growing reckless in his sullen vindictiveness while the inner struggle was evident in strange moments of aberration. A gloominess was gathering in his befuddled brain. This greatly puzzled Sykes and alarmed him as well. He watched like a spider in his lair.

Suddenly he leaned forward. A change had come over the farmer. McClure sat in his place, his head resting heavily upon his left hand. His cards lay upon the table before him face up. The game was forgotten. His eyes were reading the contents of a half-emptied glass with a stare repellent in its fierce amazement. Holding the glass tightly in his right hand he trained bulging eyes on some sight within.

At that moment Rob McClure was a physical wreck rolling helplessly on a rough sea. At best the conscience of the man was atrophied. Now it was incapable as well. The countenance, spacious with a native bigness, was marred by the double bestiality of bibber and rogue. The rudderless mind was mighty with unleashed desire. Amid the wreck of faculties sat the will, an ominous thing living, uncontrolled, with strength unimpaired, ready to strike adder-like in any direction.

Oblivious of the commotion of the game he beheld the figment of his drugged brain rising to view in the glass of drink. His face grew black with an anger horrible to behold. Amid the gleam of the liquor two faces took nebulous shape, growing in definition the longer he watched. At length they rose into view through the bubbles and froth. They vanished magically only to reappear with a tripled vividness of shape. They were living faces, of beautiful women sorrowful with a gentle reproach that stirred some tender, sleeping thing within him, while at the same instant it bated the savage beast glaring out of his eyes. As he looked, one instant fearful, the next enraged, the tender thing was suddenly crushed and the beast sprang from his lair. A wild vengefulness gleamed in his eyes as he sprang to his feet with a weird cry. Swinging his arm aloft he hurled the glass crashing upon the table before him.

"Ha!" he cried laughing horribly. "That will shut your blankety eyes."

Cunningly he searched the ring of startled faces. As he looked something clicked in the brain and the hallucination passed. His face resumed its normal expression, though an inkling of what he had just done remained dimly with him.

The others sprang to their feet in alarm, striking sudden attitudes of defense. An instant's contemplation disclosed to all his drunken state. His eyes were fixed curiously upon the shivered glass. A chorus of raillery broke out. But McClure did not smile. His face was dark.

"What the — —?" jollied Snoopy Bill.

Stepping to the door he stooped down and yelled through the keyhole:

"Hi you, Louie! No more strong stuff for McClure. He's seeing 'em. Bring a tray of lemonade."

McClure was in an unfortunate mood for the jibe. Stung by the roar of applause he leaped at Snoopy Bill in swift reprisal. Gripping him savagely by the throat he applied a strangle clutch. Snoopy's head bobbed back and he sank to the floor with blackening face. With shouts of alarm the others sprang toward the two men. Tearing away McClure's deadly grasp they pinned him to the floor. The struggle aided him to recover his mental poise. Looking up at them with a sane glance he said quietly:

"I'm through. Let me up."

Released, he regained his feet and resumed his chair.

Snoopy Bill's face was livid as he sank panting into his place. Into his eyes crept a vengeful light. He glanced sullenly about. He, too, had imbibed over freely. As he recovered the sense of outrage deepened and he proceeded to wreak immediate revenge. With the slyness of the inebriate he reached out and seized his glass. Fixing direful eyes on McClure he drew back his hand. But the murderous throw was interrupted. His wrist was suddenly caught in the vise-like grip of Sykes' long fingers.

"Better not, Bill," he admonished in a low voice. "Rob is dead drunk. Don't even know he fouled you. If you let him have that you'll be up against murder."

"He's a blankety coward," was the angry retort. "I'll get him yet. Watch me bust up this gang. By the blankety blank I'll tip Pullar himself."

Above the growls this threat produced rose the voice of Sykes roaring blasphemously at Swale who stood in the open door with mouth agape.

"You bottle washing smuggler!" he cried. "Fill up a tray of your dummest swill and hand it out on the double quick. No more poison or we'll blow you up."

Satisfied that the brawl was over Swale disappeared with the desired alacrity.

McClure's assault had tapped a smoldering mine. Though the game was resumed neither McClure nor Snoopy Bill evinced any interest, while the latter continued to breathe vengeance. Beside him sat Ford who too was showing little interest in the cards.

"Come, Ford!" challenged Snoopy Bill in a stage whisper. "I'll stump you to split on the hounds. I'm quitting."

"Cut the ragging!" called Sykes appeasingly. "This bad stuff all comes from drinking Swale's rotten whiskey. Here comes the best ever."

Swale appeared with a loaded tray. The glasses were passed around.

"Keep it!" said Snoopy Bill. "I tell you I'm quitting."

"Me too," said Nick Ford, pushing his glass away. "I reckon I'm with Bill," said he rising. "This gang's never been right. But it hit the rocks good and hard about the time Hank Foyle blew in. I know I ain't a Sunday-school teacher

179

but I've felt like a skunk since that steal of Pullar's farm. I've a sneaking idea there's some scurvy game on right now. Rolling an old man is bad enough but I draw the line at fouling a woman. I'm through."

Nick's words had a startling effect. The drinkers paused in their act of tossing the glass. There was a passage of swift glances between Sykes and McClure. The hush of a deep calm fell on the room, broken by a wild laugh from Snoopy Bill.

"Keep it up, old top!" he shouted, slapping Ford on the back. "Cough it out. Spit up the facts. We'll enjoy 'em."

Ford gave a knowing smirk.

"No, Bill," was his insinuating reply. "I ain't telling all I know. I'll let it off at the regular time."

For McClure and Sykes his words had a disquieting significance. How much did Ford know? Beyond all doubt he had an inkling of the facts.

"None of this little party know what Nick is raving about," said Sykes. "Nick's had a peculiar dream. Louie's poison got him a little differently from Rob. Let us forget the gab and every man hit the bottom of his glass. There's a tankful left. Watch us touch the high spots in this little game."

He pointed to the cards.

There was a roar of applause.

"No you don't," said Nick determinedly. "It's bye, bye, boys, for me. I'm taking a walk to myself."

"Take me along," cried Snoopy Bill, rising and joining him.

The gang watched the two delinquents lock arms and pass out into the barroom. No man made a move to obstruct them. Any such attempt would have been organized by either McClure or Sykes and for some reason they were silent.

With the game broken up the party went out.

"Come over to the office," whispered Sykes to McClure and Foyle. "Ford's next our game. We'll have to finish with a spurt if we are to pull off a win."

The interview lasted a long time. They had barely entered upon it when a shadow crept up and hung low near the window. With surprising temerity the stealthy visitant lighted a cigarette. In the light of the match appeared the dark visage of Nick Ford. He had sprung a bluff on the plotters, basing his charge on a phrase or two he had overheard. His guess had been shrewd. Satisfied that some conspiracy was afoot he decided to shadow the three men with the result that he now sat at the window listening with alert ears to the conversation going on within. He caught significant parts of their talk, enough to discover that some scheme was being concocted against the little school-teacher. He listened breathlessly in effort to learn complete details, but without success.

"Hang my ears!" was his impatient whisper. "Why can't I get it all?"

He had learned enough, however, to present him with a serious challenge.

"They've got me!" he whispered half fearfully. "Sykes has piles of money. If I chuck him he'll break me sure."

Hearing signs of a break-up of the party he stole away to his home debating the momentous demand the facts he had learned now suddenly made upon his conscience. It was easier to threaten to split on the gang than to come through with the threat, for Nick Ford was no squealer. It was dawn before he arrived at a conclusion. Finally he decided.

"Ah, Brubbie!" he breathed softly. "For her sake I'll do it. She saved you from the wolves. Yes, I'll do it. I'll let Ned Pullar know all."

XXIII

THE ADVENTURE AT THE BRIDGE

The morning following her interview with Ned, Mary elected to follow the round-about route of the Buffalo paths. She had a desire to flee the highway and sequester herself in the friendly silences. The flashing June morning was zestful with the humours of capricious little winds that pressed refreshingly on cheeks and lips and curled the brown hair about her temples. She was gratefully aware of all this caressing though looking out on the Valley with solemn eyes.

She was deep in the cogitations that pressed her continually when she realized that Bobs had halted of his own accord on the bald peak.

Below her the lake lay a glistening quietude in the verdant lap of the Valley. Vagrant breaths of tiny squalls dimpled the water here and there shading it with fleeting frowns. Beneath her the Storm Rock hung on the glassy sheet suspended between two skies. Cottonwoods and ragged oak formed an inviting bower. The island so lonely and silent had an unusual attraction for her.

"You dear little covert," she whispered. "How I should like to hide in you to-day!"

With a sigh she turned Bobs down the hill and into

Willow Glade where she must perforce halt again and muse in the precious nook with its haunting memories.

Throughout the day the children of The Craggs wondered at the frequent periods of preoccupation that would creep over their usually so attentive teacher. They were deeply touched by the singular gentleness with which she resumed the task. For all their mute sympathy the hours lagged strangely.

Nick Ford wasted no time in addressing himself to the task he had resolved upon. It is hard to travel back over the devious way one has come when that way has been too devious. To carry out his resolution would involve a divulging of most unpleasant facts. He knew of the intimate relations of Mary and Ned and trusted to Ned finding some way of foiling the designs of the plotters once he was acquainted with the fact that there was a plot. Hitching his horse he set out for the homestead with laudable dispatch.

He was bowling along, passing through a bluff not far from his destination when a shadow darted out of the trees ahead and his horse stopped abruptly. His attention was directed to the unusual movements at his horse's head when he felt a strong hand close tightly on his arm. Turning with an exclamation of surprise he looked into the grinning countenance of Reddy Sykes.

"Good-day, Nick!" was the quiet greeting. "Making a little morning run, eh?"

"Hello, Sykes!" he replied innocently. "What are you doing here?"

Sykes grinned afresh.

"Let it out, Nick," was the reply. "You're heading for

Pullar's. We've been waiting for you. I saw the yellow streak in you last night. We decided to head you off. You spoke about skunks in your little spiel. You're right and we've trapped the same polecat this morning."

At the words he dragged the other from the vehicle. Realizing his helplessness in the powerful hands of Sykes Nick decided to submit quietly to the will of his captor. Taking him into the trees Sykes sought to force a confession. But he found Nick had no particular use for free speech just then.

"Hide his horse and rig in the bluff," directed Sykes, addressing Foyle. "We'll gag this scab and hitch him to a tree for the present. If I make the get-away you can send somebody in to let him go."

In the depths of the bluff they gagged him and tying his hands behind his back strapped him to a big tree with his leather lines. Satisfied of the security of their prisoner they slipped quietly out of sight.

During the noon hour Ned joined Mary in another ride in which arrangements were perfected for their sudden nuptials. Resting in his arms at parting she looked up into his eyes.

"I am looking forward to our ride to-morrow, Ned," said she. "But how I should have delighted to set out on the great adventure from the doorstep of Mother and Dad!"

"Keep them back, Mary!" enjoined Ned cheeringly as he saw the tears shine in her eyes. Wrapping his sheltering arms about her he whispered the optimism of his great heart into her fluttering spirit.

"In our heart of hearts, Mary," said he, "we both deplore this premature wedding. But it is the only sane thing for us to do. Your mother will agree with us when you tell her to-night. She will bless us. It is the one way of assuring your protection. I believe another desirable and most wonderful result will follow. It will break the spell Sykes has cast over your father. A complete severance with Sykes and the crash of his house of cards will restore your father to you clothed and in his right mind."

At the words Ned felt the pressure of dear lips on his.

"Thank you, Ned!" were her happy words. "That is beautiful of you. And you do not hate Father after all his injustice?"

"No, Mary, I pity him. It is after all his greater misfortune."

"Good-bye," said she at last. "It is very hopeful after all. Meet me at the Buffalo Peak in the morning and we'll ride away into the days of our happy dreams."

Ned watched from the edge of the trees until the small

white figure disappeared within the schoolhouse. He was troubled as she vanished from sight. It occurred to him that she was very frail and lonely. He had a powerful impression that he should ride through the Valley with her in the evening as she returned to her home. He had proposed accompanying her to the Peak at least, but she had demurred. It was better that they should not be seen together. There were eyes that would draw pertinent conclusions that might wreck everything. Reluctantly he turned Darkey into the trail leading to the homestead.

The last few minutes with Ned greatly lightened Mary's spirits. She felt that a wise providence was guiding them. On the heels of her great depression there followed the ecstasy of a greater hope. Even storm-clouds show a silver edge at times.

Shortly after four Bobs and his rider set out for home. The day had been bright, but as the afternoon sped away a belt of blue clouds appeared in the north. From distant bluffs came the murmurous roar of a rising breeze. As she topped a ridge gusts of cold wind swept up behind her and rushed past, imbuing Bobs with the storm panic. He scurried down the trail at a spanking canter. Very soon they rode over the crest of the Cut and down into its sheltering trees. She was riding along immersed in her momentous reflections when the sudden pricking forward of Bobs' ears recalled her to the task of guiding him down the ravine. The cause of his interest she discovered in a vehicle ahead. It was slowly threading the Cut, evidently on its way to Pellawa. She was rapidly overhauling it. While conjecturing the personnel of its passengers it wheeled out of sight about a sharp curve of the hill. She followed, cantering a moment later into a narrowed pocket of the dip. She slowed her horse, for before her the road ran over a pretty bridge, scarcely wide enough for comfort in passing a carriage. The equipage had stopped upon the bridge, crowding close to one side, leaving thus plenty of room for her to pass. Sending Bobs ahead she walked him upon the bridge. As she drew abreast of the vehicle she was startled to recognize Chesley Sykes. An alarm leaped into her breast at meeting him there, for the gulch was deep and thickly wooded. It was a hidden bit of road.

Lifting his hat casually, Sykes addressed her in a friendly voice.

"Good-day, Miss McClure! An unexpected meeting!"

As he spoke, Bobs came to an abrupt stop. Mary glanced ahead. Foyle stood in their path, his hands grasping the bridle rein. Instantly the girl realized an ambuscade. With a low, frightened cry she plunged the spurs into Bobs' flanks. Blocked in front he reared, tossing his head. His wild leap lifted Foyle and threw him over the railing of the bridge. A second leap and he snapped the rein out of Foyle's hands, dropping him into the water beneath. He had shaken one assailant, however, only to be confronted by another.

"Do not be alarmed, Mary," called Sykes, as he grasped the bridle. "No harm will come to you." With Bobs plunging violently, the girl drew the automatic.

"Let go," was her stern command, "or I'll shoot."

"Blaze away, Mary!" was the cool reply, as he dodged for shelter behind Bobs' head.

Unhesitatingly the girl pulled and the gun spat its stream of lead. In the confusion of the leaping horse and her dodging target with the effort to sit her saddle, the balls went wide. Not all, however, for twice came the soft wheeze

187

of ball piercing flesh. As the balls went home, Sykes cried out, though his vigour remained unimpaired. Aware that the clip was empty she dropped the gun and addressed herself to sitting the saddle and urging Bobs in his furious struggles to free himself.

Snorting in terror, the horse leaped into the ditch, dragging Sykes with him into the trees. Plunging violently the horse galloped up the hillside through the grove. Mary kept her seat, Bobs dodging in wild plunging leaps among the trunks, until a low limb swept across their path. She could not avoid it and it caught her full in the face, sweeping her from the saddle. The powerful rebound of the strong branch flung her to the ground, where she lay quiet, a bit of white in the shrubs.

Relieved of her weight and still further terrorized, Bobs tore free from Sykes and whirling about, dashed down the Cut. Running quickly to where the still figure lay in the underbrush, Sykes picked it up in his arms and carried it into a thicket of great trees. At that instant Foyle ran up.

"Got the girl!" he applauded.

"Catch that horse," directed Sykes. "If he gets away he'll bring a nest of hornets about our ears. Run the carriage out of sight until we are ready. We made some change in our plans this morning. We are crossing the lake to Magee's Cove. The horses are waiting there. It saves us a ten-mile run about the frequented Pellawa end. The boat is ready near Grant's Landing. I am making a further change in our plans. McClure thinks we are taking the Limited for the West. Instead we are making a bee-line for Uncle Sam's the instant we reach the Cove. The plucky chit got me twice in the right arm. Only flea bites, but they are messing me up rather for a crowded Pullman. Hold the carriage ready.

You'll never catch that broncho."

Foyle hastened away to do Sykes' bidding.

As Sykes looked upon the face so cruelly torn he was touched. He passed his hand over his brow irresolute. Only a moment and the compunction vanished. Shutting his jaw he muttered in determination:

"I've got you at last, Mary, and you stay with me. Nothing in God's world will take you from me—and live."

XXIV
THE STORM ROCK

Hour succeeded hour with snail-footed pace as Nick Ford stood lashed to his tree. He fought with his gag but it was jammed firmly into his mouth and held with tight wrapped bands. The coils of the stout leather reins swathed him securely to the tree. At noon he heard Ned ride by and repass on his way home again. The rider was scarcely thirty yards away. He made a fresh fight to free himself, but without avail. He had ceased to struggle long before Mary cantered by on Bobs as she set out for home. A pang smote the man as he realized that he had failed to warn her of her danger. As the sound of the horse's hoofs died away a strange emotion shook him. Weak from his struggles and the numbing pressure of his lashings, a pathetic sense of guilt crept accusingly over him. Big tears oozed out and rolled down his cheeks. Half crazed, he prayed wild prayers that the girl might escape the evil fate lurking on her trail.

An hour passed and he heard a voice call through the

trees. Some urchin was seeking his cows. From the sound of the boy's approach he was coming straight for him. He was very near. Would he penetrate the bluff? The spot was quiet. Evidently the boy listened, but no sound occurring to attract his curiosity, he turned, whistling away, essaying some other quarter. Then happened a surprising thing. He had made but a few steps through the grass when Nick's horse lifted a sonorous whinny. Nick fervently blessed him for the intervention. It sounded like the sweetest music. The boy halted as if shot and whirling about ran into the bluff. He found the horse and vehicle at once and, a moment later, the man. Alarmed at first he retreated, but in a little set busily to work releasing the captive. In a very short time Nick was free.

"You are a good boy," said he gratefully as he made swift preparations for the ride to the homestead. "I was tied to that tree by a couple of scamps. I'll let you know all about it again. Just now I am in a great hurry to let Ned Pullar know, for he is mighty interested. Many thanks, lad. Bye, bye."

The boy gazed with astonished eyes as the man leaped on the bare back of his horse and galloped through the trees.

Nick soon clattered into the Pullar yard. At the sound of the horseman Ned and his father stepped out of the stable. The sight of the rider and his evident excitement filled Ned with foreboding.

"Why the rush, Nick?" said he as he ran up.

"Listen hard, Ned," was the swift reply. "Get your bronc. I can talk while you saddle. I hit out this way this morning to let you know, but Sykes and Foyle copped me in the bluff near the school. You're up against blankety hard luck. That deal of Foyle's was a frame-up. I was in it and helped the gang dope your old man. I'm squealing now because you've got the whitest little girl in the West and you'll have to burn the trail if you are going to save her from Reddy Sykes. McClure's bloods are waiting somewhere over the lake to run them to Whytewold. There they take the Limited for God knows where. You may be able to overhaul them, for this wind is mussing up the lake something fierce and they'll lose a couple of hours scooting around the west end. Take a look at Grant's Landing on the go-by."

By the time Nick uttered the last words Ned was in the saddle.

"Thank you, Nick," was his grateful cry as he flashed away.

"We'll follow him," cried Edward Pullar, as he watched the flying horseman vanish at the end of the lane. "Sykes is a dangerous man and the lad has nothing but his bare hands."

Leaning low over Darkey's neck, Ned heartened the lithe brute with the courage of his voice. As they flew along, the school gleamed down a vista. The memory of their last moments together, of the small white figure so lonely and beset, swept him with an agony of apprehension. Though his horse was skimming the trail with the speed of a swallow, their pace seemed laggard to the anguished rider and he plunged in his spurs. Smitten with fear, the animal leaped ahead at breakneck speed. Instantly Ned realized the wantonness of the act. Pulling gently he called penitently into the black ears:

"Forgive me, Darkey. I was cruel. I will do it no more. But carry me fast, lad."

The kind tone soothed the horse and he settled into a steady stride that devoured the miles. Overhead a change had taken place unnoticed by Ned in the hurry-skurry of his start. The belt of blue clouds had spread over the sky. Above was the explosion and flame of the breaking storm, about him the whirl of the wind and enveloping clouds of dust. It was a wild race through the hurricane to the brow of the Northwest Cut. Recklessly they dashed down the ravine, the sound of the pounding hoofs lost in the roar of the tempest. The dense cloud masses flung over them the shadow of a deep twilight.

Bursting from the Cut he halted on the crown of the slope. Below was the lake, a frowning gloom, horrible with the white fangs of the storm caps. High over the Storm Rock rose an ominous cloud of spray. Above the hiss of the whistling wind he could hear the low moan of writhing waters.

Swiftly he read the turbid surface, tracing the shore line now scarcely distinguishable in the brown murk. Near at hand was Grant's Landing. He started as he detected upon it a group of people. They were looking out into the lake. At sight of them, there came to him an augury of evil. With a heavy foreboding he sent his horse thundering down the slope. Leaping from the saddle he ran in among the watchers. In the uproar they had not heard him ride up.

"There is something wrong!" cried a fearful voice. "They are drifting. They will strike the rock."

He recognized the voice of Margaret Grant.

Her father was the first to discover his presence.

"Aye, lad! Is it you? 'Tis terrible distress we are in. McClure's bairn is oot on the fell water."

He pointed to the foam-streaked lake.

"Where are they?" shouted Ned.

Margaret heard his voice.

"Ned, Ned!" she cried, running to him. "Mary's out on the lake with Sykes and Foyle. There they are."

Straining his eyes he followed her hand. The boat was far out, visible only in fleeting glimpses when riding the crest of a wave. They were running before the wind, bearing down on the Storm Rock. Should the boat strike, it would be crushed like an egg-shell. They were now so close no escape was possible. It was but a matter of moments.

As the terrible truth came home to Ned, he stood motionless, impotent, looking with blanching face on the impending tragedy. A great sob rolled up his breast. He wanted to scream a warning over the chaos of wind and flood. Suddenly it seemed to him but a little way to Mary after all. Only the threatening chasm of the malignant waters. Should it keep them apart? He smiled that strange, innocent smile that came out somewhere from the indomitable depths of him. He would take up the gauge of the malign thing grinning at him out there in the gloom. He would swim to the rock. Running far up the shore he divested himself of boots, coat and vest and threw himself on the rollers.

Charley Grant had followed him, thinking he had espied some means of rescue. As he saw him plunge into the lake he shouted wildly:

"Come back, mon! Ye're daft to reesk it. Ye'll perish, lad."

But Ned could not hear him.

To the little company upon the landing it was a moment of horror. Their fearful interest alternated between the daring swimmer and the boat careering upon the rock.

"Mother! They are striking!" cried Margaret in a voice of

awe.

As she was speaking the boat rose high, poised a moment on the black waters, then vanished.

All eyes were strained to snatch a glimpse of the unfortunate craft. But no vestige of it could they discover.

"They are gone, Mother! Gone!" moaned the girl, hiding her face in her mother's breast.

"Can you see the lad?" called the mother, her vision blurred in tears.

Shading his eyes, Charley Grant searched the waves.

"Aye, aye! I see him yet," was the relieved cry.

For a few minutes they were able to see the head of the swimmer bob about on the tossing flood. Then it, too, vanished in the ominous gloom.

Flung high on a hissing breaker, Ned saw the boat strike and go out like the snuffing of a light. For a moment his heart seemed to hold its beat and he lay weak and helpless in the trough of the wave. Then he prayed as men do when they come to grips with death. There came a response. A new vigour flooded his body and with strokes of powerful sweep, he swam on toward the rock. It was now down wind and he made straight for it, taking the chance of being dashed upon its granite face. Watching with eagle eye he bided his time, keeping his course dead upon the rock's centre. As it loomed above a huge swell lifted him. Blinded with spray he lay on the breaker awaiting the onset. It flung him on the rock with the catapult of its snapping crest. Holding out his hands he sought to ward the crash from his head. His strong arms took the impact, the bones of his shoulders creaking under the strain. Withal his head struck a jagged point. Sense reeled and he rolled hither and thither, like a log on the churning wash. By a mighty effort he righted himself and feeling a sharp edge, clung to it with all the strength of his powerful clutch. Caught in the lateral flow of the split wave he was carried to the side. Clinging to the jutting ledge by a sort of hand-over-hand movement, he was floated around the rock. So far was he borne that he could see the quieter waters of the lee shelter. Ten feet more and he would be there. Then ensued a fierce struggle. The subsiding wave sought to drag him back into the lake. With hands torn on the ragged edges he fought to retain his precarious hold. A moment's baffling balancing and the wave passed on. Quickly he drew himself into a shielding niche. There he rested, breathing heavily. In a little he would search the rock.

Clambering up the side he attempted to scan the upper surface, at the same instant lifting a shout. But the wind snatched the cry from his lips and flung him down the rock. The brief glance had disclosed to him an astonishing thing, however. The rock was as bare as the nude surface of a melting berg. The cottonwoods and their patch of clinging turf had been swept away, leaving only the naked contour of the original monolith. The emptiness of the place smote him with a dread fear. Climbing cautiously into the teeth of the storm he shouted again, throwing a name into the uproar. But the wind hurled him back once more. As he caught his feet he was thrilled to hear a shout. It came from the spot where he had struck. Shouting with the full power of his throat he clambered to the edge. A heavy billow had dashed upon the reef, flinging aloft a cloud of spray. Something at the base of the cloud held his fascinated gaze. Fighting the buffeting deluge he sought to visualize the thing before him. In the blur of the gray mist he thought he defined a phantom figure balanced on the wave-battered edge of the rock. One arm hung strangely at its side, while the other was lifted in effort to maintain a footing upon the slippery surface. As he looked there was a thunderous roar. An enormous wave had rolled up. Lifting the struggling figure on its foaming crest it whisked it across the rock. In the swift passage it fought to catch its feet, succeeding for the briefest instant only. Upon the lee edge of the rock the figure stood up in the wave and lifted a warding hand. But it could not breast the whelming flow and was swept like a chip into the darkness beyond. As the figure vanished into the mists there broke on Ned's ear a weird shout. It sounded like the mocking laugh of a fiend.

A shudder swept over the hearer. The phantom was Chesley Sykes.

While the horror of the moment was still heavy upon him he heard what seemed like an answering shout. The quality of it thrilled him, for it was a woman's cry. Looking over the bare surface he was amazed to detect the rump stump of the ragged oak. Low at its base lay a clinging shadow. Megaphoning with his hands he shouted with all his might. He was electrified to catch a distinct reply. The voice? He knew it. A wild joy surged through him. It was Mary. She was clinging to the oak.

Swamped by the panic of the mad moment he was about to dash over the rock, when there flashed before him the fate of that phantom figure. He restrained the wild desire and studying the rock saw that by a detour of the lee side he could reach to within a few yards of the oak. A swift run over a dangerous buttress and he would be with Mary. Fearful that the tremendous waves might wrench her free, he worked about the rock with furious impatience, making the circuit without mishap. With a sharp flit he was over the buttress.

The girl was plainly nearing the limit of her endurance and looked into his face with a half-fearful wonder as he lifted her in his arms.

"Ned!" she cried, "you are not Sykes? I thought I heard him cry a little ago with such a terrible, screaming laugh."

"It is Ned, dear," was his cry as he placed her more securely against the oak. "Rest a little. You are very weak but you will recover shortly."

Kneeling upon the rock, he took the oak in his hands and, turning his back to the storm, crouched above her, so shielding her from the pounding waves and the chill of the hurricane. Huge billows continued to deluge the rock and their smashing force soon began to tell. She discovered before he did that his strength was going. After an exhausting struggle with an unusually powerful wave, she called to him.

"Let me go, Ned. You cannot stand much more. That last almost swung you about the tree."

"I will crouch lower," said Ned. "The wind will subside soon. Then I can carry you to that shelter under the ledge."

Thrilled by the magic of her clinging touch he would not acknowledge the fearful inroads the long struggle had made on his strength. Now he knew no terror. True, a dizziness would confuse him at times on the heels of the heavier swells, but he clutched the tree and clung till it passed.

"You cannot stand many more," cried the girl fearfully. "Leave me. You can still make the shelter or swim——"

"Hush, Mary!" was the cheery reply. "You would rob me

197

of the happiest moment I have ever known. We'll stick together, dear. We are good for a lot of roughing yet."

"You will not leave me, Ned?"

"Not ever, Mary."

"Ned, dear heart!" was the caressing cry. "This is a wonderful moment. It is worth all the cruelty of these last, long months and the horror of this terrible day. You are the dearest pal."

"Pal?" cried Ned, looking into the dark eyes. "What pals we'll be!"

That they were tortured with the smiting waves and facing death with each succeeding roller, only enhanced the supreme joy of their confession.

"We are going to get out of this all right," said Ned, as he breathed heavily from a battle with a mighty wave. "You hardly think it possible, little one, you have been so broken by this battering storm. But we'll beat it all, water, wind and human guile."

Suddenly he straightened up and placed hand to ear.

"Listen, Mary!" he called. "Can you not hear it? There are voices coming up the wind."

They listened. From the lee of the rock came a faint shout. Together they replied. Again the shout and this time astonishingly close.

"There is a boat near," cried Ned. "I caught a glimpse of it through the spray."

With the sudden prospect of rescue, hope leaped up afresh. A new courage entered their minds and a strange new strength their bodies. Both were opportune, for now they entered upon a desperate struggle with successions of formidable waves. They had nearly passed when the black dizziness, that of late had been recurring with alarming frequency, fell suddenly upon Ned. Fainting under the exertion he sank. His head hung over the edge of the rock and only the super-human efforts of his companion prevented him from plunging headlong into the lake.

"Mary!" he cried as consciousness came dimly back. "I have been asleep. Did the roller beat me that time?"

"You were nearly gone," cried the girl faintly.

"How did you ever hold me, dear?"

"I don't know, Ned. But you are here. You cannot stand another. Is the boat near?"

The girl's voice had a terror in it that smote Ned with pity.

The boat at that moment rode through the choppy waves, to shelter at the base of the rock. The instant the prow struck a great figure leaped out of her and scrambled up over the ledge. As it straightened up for the dash to the oak, Ned was amazed to behold the face of Rob McClure. It was distorted by a terror born of no sense of physical danger. There was a poignant agony in his voice as he cried:

"Mary, Mary! Are you here?"

"She is here and safe," shouted Ned in reply.

Stooping down Ned exerted all his strength and lifting the small form, placed her in her father's arms.

"Brace against that stump," cried Ned as a billow hit them.

"Daddy! You have come!" cried the girl as she nestled in her father's arms. Upon her face was the look of wonder inexplicable with which she had greeted Ned. In Ned's eyes was a wonder even greater. He was pondering this astounding enigma when a cloud swept over his mind with a horrible enveloping and he fell on the rock. A fresh wave clutched him as two shadows darted to where he lay.

199

"Just in time!" cried the voice of Andy Bissett, as he fought the wave for possession of the inert form.

"Shure, 'tis full spint is the lad," was the response of Easy Murphy. "There's been a divil of a scrap wid wind and wathurr on this bauld-headed stone."

"It has been a wonderful fight," agreed Andy as they got their burden safely out of the clutch of the breakers.

"Thrue, me hearty! And the swate colleen wuz worth it, begobs."

In the boat were Lawrie and Jean Benoit and another— Foyle. He was haggard and dishevelled and silent.

Securing their precious salvage the crew explored the rock, shouting loudly in hope of another survivor, but the only reply was the uproar of the tempest. Convinced that no living thing remained they shoved off and ran for the southeast shore.

XXV
THE EMPTY SADDLE

After tearing free from Sykes, Bobs galloped through the woods till with true broncho instinct he circled to the trail and shot post haste for home. After a time his terror passed and he reduced his speed to a comfortable canter, then to a trot and finally to a walk. Loitering leisurely along the way he nibbled choice tufts of grass.

When the hour of Mary's home-coming arrived and there was no sight of her along the Valley trail, Helen McClure grew mildly anxious. With the passage of an hour and still no sign she became alarmed and consulted McClure. He betrayed no evidences of anxiety and endeavoured to calm the agitated woman. It was during the furious outbreak of the storm that she saw the riderless horse trot swiftly down the lane. A dread seized her and she called to Rob.

He was seated in his office, his eye fixed in remarkable tenderness upon the two faces that for the last few days had haunted him. The anguished tone of his wife smote him and a wave of shame passed over his face. He dropped his head upon his hand. A curious enervation sapped his strength. That cry with its tender distress broke something hard within him. He could not lift up his head. The fact of the bribe and its mighty lure were forgotten. In the space of one marvellous instant he became humane. In upon him surged an overwhelming solicitude for Mary's safety. Endearing memories rushed upon him. His dishonour and the pathos of Mary's betrayal cried out in the smitten cry of his wife. Remorse and contrition were strangely confused in the mind that refused to work with its accustomed celerity. Grimly he reflected that the office of the blue automatic was desirable. Opening the drawer he thrust his hand within. The gun was gone. Who could take it? His wife? Mary? Ah, it was Mary. He brushed his brow in a troubled gesture. In upon the deepening gloom burst a disquieting fear.

"Rob!" came the cry again in a low frightened tone. "Bobs has come home without Mary. He must have thrown her. Perhaps she is injured or—killed."

"Tut, tut, Helen!" was his answer. "She is not hurt. Have no fear for Mary. She is too good a rider. She is walking along the trail."

"But it is so late," objected the mother anxiously.

Together they went out to where Bobs was refreshing himself at the trough. A quick examination of the horse aroused in McClure a new uneasiness. The bridle was torn and the rein gone. Suddenly Helen discovered something Rob hoped she would not see.

"Here are marks of the spurs," called his wife. "Mary never uses these terrible things."

She pointed to red dabs along the flank.

Passing about the horse Rob discovered a bloody mark on Bobs' white hip that aroused a panic in his own breast. Beneath the smear of blood there was no wound. His wife detected what he was looking at.

"That cannot be from the spurs," she cried in a stricken voice. "Mary has met with an accident, that she made a wild effort to escape."

She sought his eye.

"Listen, Helen!" said he in a low tone, transfixed by her compelling glance. "Do not jump to wild conclusions and believe all I say. You may never forgive me. You must believe me. Mary is not hurt. She has gone with Chesley Sykes. They will come back again. He was to intercept her on her way from school. It was all arranged. I gave my consent and Hank Foyle was to help him out. He will marry our girl."

His confession had come in a slow, passionless voice. As the truth dawned upon her the blood receded from her face, leaving her white and haggard. Old age seemed to have fallen magically upon her. Her lips moved as if to speak, but no sound issued forth. She reeled as if struck. Rob threw his arms about her. At his touch she stood erect and rigid. Thrusting him gently from her, she turned away with a low moan.

With bowed head he led Bobs to the stable and went

slowly, dazedly into the house. All within was quiet. The stillness troubled him. His wife had secluded herself. He called her name but no answer came back. Making a swift search he found her at length in Mary's room. She knelt before the bed fondling some trinkets she had spread out upon the counterpane. Her eyes were fixed upon a tiny photograph. It was a likeness of Mary when a babe.

"Ah, poor little baby!" she whispered. "They have broken your dear little heart."

As Rob watched the stricken creature an exquisite pain stabbed his own soul. Walking over to her he threw his great arms about her.

"Listen, Helen," said he brokenly. "Before God Almighty I'll bring Mary back to you."

She seemed not to hear him.

Rising he walked out.

Hitching up his team he pushed them at a terrific pace for Magee's Cove. He arrived at the Cove thankful to find that the bloods were still there. He was ahead of the boat. He soon discovered it out in the lake and in grave peril. Before he could fully realize the situation the boat crashed upon the Storm Rock. In the closing dusk he fancied he saw a gleam of white upon the rock. Obsessed with a wild hope that it was Mary he sent his horses at a gallop to Magee's and got out his big steam launch just as Andy and his party came up, bent on the same purpose. Supplementing the engine with oars they drove for the rock, picking Foyle up near shore. The tale he gave them impelled them to heroic effort and they fought their way steadily toward the rock. When near they discovered two figures, taking them for Mary and Sykes. Their astonishment knew no bounds when they found out that Mary's companion was Ned.

The return was effected easily and speedily. The boat was cutting through the breakers not far from shore when Lawrie, who was in the prow, gave a peculiar cry and signalled the reversal of the engine. It was called forth by an object rocking amid the flotsam. Instantly the boat was halted and backed to where the object lay in the water.

"My God!" cried Easy Murphy, as they rode alongside. "It's Sykes, poor divil!"

At the words a moan came from somebody. Through McClure passed a shudder and he drew Mary close to him. Producing a rope they attached it to the gruesome thing out in the waves and started shoreward once more.

Mary was taken direct to her home. Mrs. Grant insisted on warmth and refreshment, but Rob would hear of no delay.

"Her mother is waiting," said he, with the saddest of smiles.

The drive was accomplished at a speed that brought the bays to rest at the McClure threshold in a reek of sweat.

On that home-coming no eyes must peer. Upon Helen McClure's face lay the ineffaceable scars of her dark vigil. But her heart was healed by the miracle of the storm.

And Ned? The tonic of love and youth more than pulled him through.

XXVI
THE RED KNIGHT SINGS OF THE FAIRIES

The sun was sinking behind a sky of golden fleeces.

Through the dazzling cloud-rims streamed the lava of sunny light, flooding The Qu'Appelle with its restful glow. Below lay the lake, a rippling basin of molten gold.

Everywhere the shadowy greens of the crests were checkered with square patches of ripe wheat. Some fields were mellow for the sickle. Upon the morrow the binders would hum the overture of the harvest symphony.

Two watchers sat on the Grant lawn drinking in the liquid glow of the west. Down upon them rolled a field of Red Knight, covering the terrace to their feet. The light of a blazing summer and its dews and rains lay before them, stored in a forest of magic heads. The grain was standing thick and erect, its cream-gold surface dappled with pursuing waves of shade and shine. The eyes of the watchers rested on the sea of plumes. They were talking of it.

"Wonderful! Indeed!" exclaimed Margaret softly. "It is as wonderful as Ned and his father think it is."

"Yes!" agreed Andy. "I for one believe it will far surpass their hopes. And yet I am scarcely qualified to judge since the ride of a certain girl to the rescue of The Red Knight. His precious gold kernels were the sesame that opened her eyes. I have a natural bias toward him but he is a marvel all the same and the king of cereals. The scientists, the cereal breeders, even the millers agree with the Pullars and the farmers in pronouncing The Red Knight a wonder grain. I believe with old Edward Pullar that it will be the elixir of life to millions of farmers. It is interesting to conjure just what this will mean to the future of our country. Beyond a doubt it will draw the strong of the earth to the virile North."

Andy paused musing for a time. Then he said gently:

"There is something great, magnificently great in all

this, something that dwarfs The Red Knight himself."

At his words the girl sought her companion's eyes. Swiftly she divined his thoughts.

"You mean somebody is great, do you?" said she.

Andy nodded thoughtfully.

"Yes. There is Edward Pullar and Ned, himself, and the little mother. These dear neighbours of ours have been great in vision and patience. We have not understood. Most people about Pellawa never will. The old homestead at The Craggs has been a place of unobtrusive but astounding achievement. These quiet farmers are mighty benefactors. What farmers they are!"

"Look!" cried Margaret, suddenly pointing into the west.

Along the distant edge of the wheat were moving three shapes, black shadows of riders suspended in the amber light as they skimmed along the high shoulder of an upper bench. A moment only were they visible. Then they melted into the yellow sea.

"The McClures!" announced Margaret, a reflective light shining in her eyes. "This is Mary's first ride—since the storm. She is happy to-night."

"I am sure she is. But how do you know?" mused Andy.

"The curvetings of Bobs assured me," was the reply. "Mary is in the happy mood that inspires Bobs with a foolish notion that he has wings instead of legs and must fly away."

"Which reminds me," said Andy with a smile, "that I, too, am foolishly happy. Have you observed my grove lately? If not, better take a careful look."

Margaret followed his gesture. She saw a strange white object among the trees. Her eyes brightened, but

206

dissembling with feminine facility, she looked up in naïve curiosity.

"It is the gable of our roof," explained Andy, looking deep into the clear eyes. "I cut down that old rotten elm that you might get a glimpse of what is to be expected—of you. Hum!"

Margaret made no reply except a widening of innocent eyes.

"To resume," continued Andy. "It will be plastered before the frost; during the winter we shall finish it. Then, after seeding, some day in June——"

Andy paused. The gaze of his companion was gratifyingly intent. He waited.

"Well?" came the incurious query.

"Well!" was the deliberate reply. "What so rare as a bride in June?"

Margaret read the face above her, read it deeply, gravely, for a moment, then released an entrancing smile.

"Would you care to really know?" was her arch reply.

"Would I?"

"Then hear! It is the bold fellow who conspires with himself against her."

Edward Pullar was passing among his head-row plots, spending a busy hour in the cool of the twilight. His eyes were ashine and a cheerful humming proclaimed a happy worker, deeply in love with his work. And it was so, for was not the Red Knight scaling another wall in the grand assault? Already the aged gleaner had harvested a wealth of selected heads and the tub on the kitchen floor was the receptacle of several gallons of the astonishing brown-red

207

kernels. There was a prophetic light on the old man's face as he plucked the wonderful heads. So deep was his self-communion that he was startled when a voice called for the second time:

"Mr. Pullar!"

The voice was powerful but suppressed, its tone familiar. The old man looked up in surprise.

Before him stood Rob McClure and his wife. With instinctive gentility he doffed his hat and bowed.

"Good-evening to you, friends!" was his cordial greeting.

"Thank you for your kindness, Edward Pullar," was McClure's slow reply. "I have ridden over to see you though you may not desire conversation with me. I would not blame you — —"

Edward Pullar raised his hand.

"Hush! My friend!" he entreated gently, a brightness glowing in his eyes. "I understand all. Nick Ford has given me the tale without reserve. The past has been very dark for all of us; the expiation—costly. There are enigmas that remain unexplained but the explanation would merely satiate curiosity. It would not alter anything. We have forgotten the past. Life is new, sacredly new for Ned and me —since the storm. We want no confession, no ceaseless grieving, simply your dear friendship. We are looking ahead into the gloriously happy days. Give me your hands."

The others stepped impulsively to him and seized his hands.

"You mean it! I know you mean it!" said Rob McClure, his great eyes lingering reverently on the old man's face. "Do you know that we attempted to steal your bins of Red Knight? That we sold your farm by a devil's ruse? That we fought Ned, nine to one, with savage design to maim him for life? That we planned a terrible wrong and carry the red brand of crime? Do you..."

"Hush! My friend!" cried the old man, stemming the hot torrent of self-condemnation. "Do not recall it, I implore you. I know it all, but it is cast behind. We hold in our memories only the joys of those dark days, for there was much that was precious. Besides, there are the bairns. For their sakes and for our own I will be having you always for my friends."

"Edward Pullar!" cried the soft, thrilled voice of Helen McClure. "God will bless you for those noble words. He will nourish this dear friendship into which you are taking us."

As she spoke the moon rolled up over the prairie edge, throwing over them all a faint, rosy light through the gauzy fringe of a low cloud.

"How wonderful!" cried Helen McClure. "It is the warm light of promise."

Through the shadows of the young night came suddenly the voice of laughter, silvery as the call of a bird to its mate. It was barely audible indeed, but distinct and athrob with joy. It was Mary's voice. At the sound a wave of deep emotion swept over the three people and their hands tightened in a clinging grip.

Mary was in just the fettle Margaret had surmised. Discovering Ned busy at his binders, she had lured him with her call. In a moment he was with her and gathered her into his arms. About them flowed the light of the moon, bathing tree trunks and leaves and the rippling wheat in its soft, red shine.

"See her!" cried the girl, pointing to the glowing orb veiled in its tracery of leaves and limbs. "Have you ever seen her so benign?"

"Never!" cried Ned happily. "To-night she is witching. She is painting you with her dainty rouge, face and lips, and this soft, brown hair. In your eyes her light of wonderful old rose is the light of dear desire."

"Evidently she holds a spell," teased Mary, "and does not scruple to throw dream stuff into the foolish eyes of young farmers."

"What an occult magician she is!" cried Ned delightedly, abandoning himself to the deceit of the moment. "She has everything about us revelling. The little winds are flirting scandalously with your curls and there is a whispering music out there in the moving grain. There are voices in the wheat that haunt me. Often have I dreamed of them but never have I caught their singing until now. Something tells me you understand—you favourite sorceress of rose-light moons."

"This is our mad-moon, Ned," laughed Mary softly. "I begin to feel the strange thrill of its lunacy. This old-rose light is a glamourous thing. Put your cheek against mine, dear pal, and I'll whisper to you the secret that is throbbing in the heart of our wonderful Knight.

210

"His voices come sweetly in stealing from very far and in all their singing there is a tender tale they tell of kind eyes that glanced upon him one great day and of a gentle hand that plucked him out of the wilds and set his roots in the wise hearts of men. With a million, adoring tongues he is hymning to-night the tender spirit of Kitty Belaire. Hark to the legends he sings of the coming days! One beautiful noon your father, Ned, told me a remarkable thing. 'The Red Knight,' said he, 'will push the grain belt three hundred miles nearer the poles.' It is of this The Red Knight is whispering now. His prophetic voices are winging in from everywhere and they tell of a wondrous host trekking the illimitable plains of this magic North. Listen, Ned, and you will hear their tramp through the enchanting glow of our mad rose moon."

"I can hear it, Mary!" was the hushed reply as he nestled the brown head close. "And in all the tramping of the countless feet I hear a fairy patter like the sound of falling leaves. Are they the fragile feet of the fairy children flitting to us out of the infinite?"

"Ned, my Ned!" was the endearing cry. "The Red Knight is singing of the homes he will build in his gardens of wheat, of the tiny fairies, the little children of the plains who shall play in his gardens—in your garden, Ned, and mine."

Ned's answer was the drawing tight of his great arms and the sheltering crush of his mightier love.

A mist crept over Mary's eyes. Looking through the glad tears she whispered:

"It is the 'bestest' year we have ever seen, both for us and for—them."

Over all rose the moon, now white and serene, pouring

211

upon them the silver light of her purity.

Printed in the United States of America

www.ingramcontent.com/pod-product-compliance
Lightning Source LLC
Chambersburg PA
CBHW020617030726
47497CB00007B/2289